The Dressing Room Murder

J.S. Fletcher

Originally published 1931
Herbert Jenkins,
London, U.K.

This edition published 2023 by

OREON

an imprint of

The Oleander Press
16 Orchard Street
Cambridge
CB1 1JT

www.oleanderpress.com

ISBN: 9781915475213

A CIP catalogue record for the book
is available from the British Library.

Cover design, typesetting & ebook: neorelix

Contents

Chapter I

THE DRESSING ROOM

HATHERFORD, like most of the big North Country towns, was well supplied with clubs, political and social. There was the Conservative Club and the Liberal Club, each a headquarters of political propaganda; the Hatherford Club was a non-political, social affair. Then there were two or three sporting clubs, sacred to the racing fraternity; Labour clubs existed in every ward of the city. And tucked away in a backstreet, opening off the main square of the place, was yet another, the Hyacinth, the membership of which was strictly limited to one hundred. Viewed from without, the Hyacinth had nothing to recommend it, but seen from within it was the most comfortable and alluring resort in Hatherford. Its members — membership was difficult of attainment — formed a sort of brotherhood sworn to avoid all contentious topics; its chef was noted for his skill; everything within its luxuriously fitted rooms was of the best, and the man who was fortunate enough to once gain admittance to them felt that his day would be incomplete if it did not wind up within their portals.

On a certain November evening some few years ago three men sat at a round table in the dining room of the Hyacinth with cigars between their lips and coffee and liqueurs in front of them. One, a big, broad-shouldered man, was Marston, Chief Constable of Hatherford; another, a sharp-eyed, spectacled little person, was Grayle, police surgeon; the third was Alderman Wardle, chairman of the Watch Committee. These three were bachelors and cronies: you might have found them dining together at the Hyacinth five nights out of the seven. Between them they knew most of the police secrets of the town: Wardle, as the most elderly and a native of the city, more than the other two, who were comparatively recent comers; Marston had been there nine, Grayle seven years. But they never talked professional stuff at the Club; they got plenty of that at the City Hall, close by. And they were not talking it now.

"Doing anything tonight?" enquired Wardle as he finished his coffee. "Going anywhere?"

Marston nodded across the table at the police surgeon.

"Grayle and I," he replied, "were thinking of dropping in at the theatre to see this big chap Sir John Riversley. Never seen him, either of us — on the stage, I mean. Saw him, of course, at the City Hall today, when he lunched with the Mayor. He's playing Hamlet, and they say it's his best achievement, so far."

Wardle lighted a fresh cigar.

"Odd thing," he remarked. "Sir John's never played in Hatherford before tonight. He's been one of the three or four big world-actors for the last ten or twelve years, but this is his very first appearance in Hatherford. And yet he was born here!"

"Native, eh?" said Grayle. "Didn't know that!"

"Native. I know exactly where he was born — and all about him," replied Wardle. "For that matter I knew his father and mother. The father — "

A club steward came across the room to the Chief Constable's side.

"Wanted on the phone, Mr. Marston," he said. "Urgent!"

Marston excused himself and went out into the hall to the telephone box.

"Hullo?" he said.

There was no mistaking the agitation in the tones of the answer.

"That the Chief Constable?"

"Yes!"

"This is Gresford — manager Theatre Royal. Can you come here at once?"

"Something wrong?"

"Very wrong! Sir John Riversley. We've found him dead in his dressing room. I'm afraid it's murder!"

"Murder?"

"Looks like it! Will you come?"

"At once! Got a doctor there?"

"Yes — Feversham."

"All right — be with you in five minutes."

He shot out of the box and collared a passing page boy.

"Run out! — get me the first taxi you see — quick!"

Then he hastened back to the dining room. Something in his face made the two men he had left rise to their feet.

"What — " began Wardle.

"H'sh!" said Marston, glancing about him. "Listen! That was Gresford, the manager at the theatre. They've found Sir John Riversley dead in his dressing room — Gresford thinks it's murder. Come on — I've got a taxi outside."

The other two followed him in silence; in silence all three got into their hats and overcoats and filed out to the waiting cab.

"Theatre Royal — stage door — as fast as you can," said Marston.

The cab moved off: Wardle drew a long breath.

"Good God!" he said. "And we were just talking about him!"

Marston leaned forward and tapped Wardle's knee.

"Look here!" he said. "If this is murder, it's murder in his native town! You said you knew all about him? Tell!"

"Yes — yes — I see what you mean," replied Wardle. "Well, yes, I do know all about him — up to a certain point, that is. His father had a small business here — commission woolcomber. This chap was brought up to it; stuck to it till he was, well, perhaps twenty-two or -three. But he was always keen on acting — started with the Hatherford Amateur Dramatic Society, you know. Eventually, he decided to go on the stage, professionally. Went. Don't know how he fared at first — usual thing, I reckon; hard times, and so on. Then, you know, he suddenly blossomed out some ten or twelve years since and became world-famous. Got a knighthood last year. That's about all."

"How old is he now?" asked Marston.

"Let me think. He'll be forty-five."

"And he left the town, for the professional stage, when he was twenty-two?"

"About that."

"So that's about twenty-two or twenty-three years ago?"

"That's about it."

"Then there must be no end of people here who remember him?"

"Good Lord, yes! No end! But, as far as I can remember, he's never been back in Hatherford since he left it, until now. He's certainly never played here."

"Any relations here?"

"Can't say, definitely. The father and mother are dead, and he was an only child. There may be relations, but I don't know of — "

Grayle interrupted as the cab turned a corner.

"The news is out!" he said. "Look there!"

The street in front of the Theatre Royal was packed with people. But there was a dead silence over all of them; if they were talking, it was in whispers. And in the side street which led to the stage door there was another crowd, and its members, too, were equally silent. It was amidst an absolute silence that Marston and his companions jumped from the cab and hurried in past the doorkeeper, to encounter Gresford, the manager, white-faced and shaking. Without a word he beckoned them into an empty room close by.

"Well?" asked Marston.

"It's murder!" said Gresford miserably. "Feversham says there's no doubt of it — there can't be any doubt, either. He — Sir John, I mean — came in an hour before the performance was due and went straight to his dressing room; he'd called in earlier in the day and seen it. His dresser, Pratt, was a bit late — he came in twenty minutes after Sir John. When he entered the dressing room, he found Sir John lying over his table — he'd been stabbed to the heart, from behind. Feversham says he must have died instantaneously."

"Stabbed?" said Marston.

Gresford nodded — pointing up the passage.

"You can see for yourself," he said. "We haven't touched anything. Feversham said we mustn't — till you came. Will you come — and see?"

The three men followed the manager along the passage to the door of a room outside which stood a policeman, Dr. Feversham, and a little man who was sobbing into his handkerchief. The policeman opened the door; all but the little man went inside.

"Just as — as Pratt there, the dresser, the man who's crying outside, found it!" whispered Gresford. "Nothing's been touched, has it, doctor?"

"Nothing!" said Feversham.

Marston took the scene in at one glance. Sir John Riversley, seated at his dressing table, lay with the upper half of his body sprawled across it and with his arms thrown out; close to the fingers of one hand lay a stick of grease-paint. He was in his shirt and trousers, and there was a crimson stain on the back of the shirt, and a pool of blood on the white covering of the table. And on the floor, thrown down carelessly, was a rapier.

Marston looked round; touched Gresford's arm; whispered.

"That door? — where does it lead?"

"To the stage."

"And that?"

"Into a passage that leads round to the front of the theatre."

"No other way of getting into this room than by those doors?"

"Except by this — that we came in by. And nobody came in that way till Pratt came."

Again Marston looked round. He was searching for something — a hiding-place. But after a glance he shook his head.

"No!" he said. "Nobody could have been hidden here. Whoever it was, he came in on him by one of those doors. Well!" He turned to the two doctors. "Your job, now," he said. "You know what to do about removal, examination, and so on. Now let me see your stage-door keepers, Gresford, and the dresser. Come with me, Wardle — we can't do anything here."

Gresford led them back to the room they had first entered and called the stage-door keeper. Marston, a regular theatregoer, knew him well, and knew him, too, as a man to be trusted as regards facts.

"Did you see Sir John come in, Jenkinson?" he asked.

"I did, sir."

"What time was that?"

"Exactly six-thirty, Mr. Marston."

"Anybody with him?"

"Nobody!"

"And no one called and asked for him afterwards?"

"No, sir."

"When did Pratt come in?"

"Twenty minutes after Sir John. Of course, he ought to have been here before Sir John. He was in a state — said he'd been in a tram accident."

"Did he go straight to Sir John's room?"

"He did so! Hurried. Next instant he was back — with the news."

Marston turned to Gresford.

"Call Pratt in," he said. "Not," he added, "that he'll be able to tell us anything that we don't know. Now, Pratt," he went on as the dresser entered, "you were late in getting to your master tonight, eh? — and when you went into his dressing room you found him — as we've just seen him?"

Pratt made an attempt to stifle his sobs.

"Yes, sir," he answered. "I was late through being in a tram that broke down — my lodgings are up the Weatherfield Road, sir. When I did get here, he was — just as you saw, sir."

"There was no other person there, Pratt?"

"No, sir. Just — himself."

"Any of those doors open in the dressing room?"

"No, sir, they were all closed."

"What did you do?"

"Ran to tell Jenkinson, sir. He called Mr. Gresford."

"Sir John was staying at the Midland Hotel, wasn't he, Pratt?"

"Yes, sir — suite of rooms there."

Marston turned again to Gresford.

"I don't know anything about Sir John's private affairs," he remarked. "Was he a married man?"

Pratt answered.

"Sir John was a bachelor, sir. He'd never been married."

"Have you seen him at his rooms at the hotel since you came, Pratt?" enquired Marston. "This is Monday — I suppose he came yesterday?"

"We came along yesterday morning, sir, from Sheffield. I saw Sir John in his rooms yesterday evening for a few minutes, and again this morning for a few minutes."

"Was he alone?"

"Alone yesterday, sir, when I saw him. This morning he had two gentlemen with him. I understood that one was the Mayor — I don't know who the other was. They were having a glass of wine with him, sir."

"You didn't see him again, during the day?"

"No, sir — not until — until just now, sir." Marston took Gresford aside.

"Now," he said, "fetch Sir John's business manager."

Chapter 2

I WILL NOT SAY!

AS Gresford left the room, Jenkinson put his head in at the door, glancing at the Chief Constable.

"There's Detective Sergeant Stell outside, Mr. Marston," he said. "He wants to know if you wish him to come in?"

Marston and Wardle exchanged a swift look — Wardle nodded.

"The very man — best of the lot!" he said. "Have him in, Marston."

Marston nodded at the doorkeeper; a moment later he turned from a whispered word with Wardle to confront a young, quietly-attired, self-possessed man who entered and carefully closed the door behind him.

"I was passing," he said in level, unemotional tones. "I heard what had happened and that you were here. So I came round to the stage door."

"Quite right, Stell — you've heard, you say?" replied Marston.

Stell nodded.

"No details," he said.

"Well, it's just this," continued Marston. He went on to epitomise the main facts. "Gresford's gone for Sir John's business manager — you stay here and listen to what he has to say. When we've heard that, we'll get on to something else."

Gresford came back just then, ushering in a tall, handsome man who was obviously in great distress of mind.

"Mr. Carroll," said Gresford.

Marston wasted no time in civilities.

"Mr. Carroll. You're Sir John Riversley's business manager, I understand?" he said. "Can you tell us anything about this business — his murder? For it is murder!"

Carroll shook his head and spread his hands.

"Nothing!" he answered miserably. "I know nothing!"

"Did you see Sir John when he came in tonight?"

"I didn't!"

"Do you know when he came in?"

"Since — since his death was discovered I have heard from the stage doorkeeper that he came in at six-thirty. That was his practice — to be in his dressing room exactly an hour before the play began."

"His dresser, Pratt, ought to have been there in readiness for him, I suppose?"

"Yes — but tonight, for I should say the first time, Pratt was late. He got involved in some tram accident, he tells me."

"So that Sir John would find his dressing room untenanted, and be there alone for some fifteen or twenty minutes?"

"Yes — that would seem to be the case."

"Well now, Mr. Carroll, have you made any enquiries amongst the members of the company as to whether any of them saw Sir John after he arrived? Do you know if any of them visited Sir John in his room?"

"I've made full enquiry — of every single member of the company! After we heard the news I got the company together. No one saw Sir John after his arrival; no one entered his room."

"They gave you individual assurance of that?"

"I can't say individual assurance. I put a general question — two questions, rather — to the company. The same question you've just put to me: Had anyone seen him since he came to the theatre; had anyone been to his room for anything? No one had seen him; no one had been to him."

"Where were you, yourself, at that time?"

"Round at the front ; at the box office. I was there, with Mr. Gresford, when the news was brought to us."

Marston considered matters during a moment's silence. He turned again to Carroll.

"Well now, Mr. Carroll, there's no doubt this is a case of murder," he said. "Sir John was run through from behind, as he sat at his table, by the rapier which we found thrown aside on the floor. Do you know anything about that rapier?"

"Yes! It was Sir John's own — he frequently wore it. It is a valuable weapon — a real Spanish blade, given to him by an admirer, some years ago. I often warned him against using it — a property sword would have done just as well. But he had a curious affection for it — whenever he played a part in which he had to use or carry a weapon of that sort he always made use of it."

"It would be lying about in his room tonight, I suppose?"

"Yes — he had no doubt taken it out of its case himself, as I've often seen him do."

"Very well — now I'm coming to the most important question of all, Mr. Carroll. What were the relations between Sir John and the members of his company?"

Carroll hesitated: it was plain that the question was not welcome to him.

"Taking it altogether, and as a rule, quite good," he answered. "He had the reputation of being very strict, something of a martinet, but everybody had a great admiration of him and was proud to play with him. He was thought to be a little close-fisted, to be sure; the fact is, he was a keen businessman and knew the value of money."

"You said 'taking it altogether and as a rule,' Mr. Carroll. Does that mean that there have been exceptions?"

"You can't avoid exceptions. I have been Sir John's business manager ever since he went into management, ten years ago. As I say, taking it altogether, his relations with his employees have been entirely satisfactory, but there have, of course, been exceptions."

Marston paused — and suddenly turned sharply on Carroll.

"Anything of that sort — lately?" he asked with emphasis on the last word. "Think, now — lately?"

Carroll lifted a hand and stroked his chin.

"You wish me to answer that?" he asked.

"In view of what's just happened," said Marston, "I do!"

"Well, there was some trouble last week, when we were playing at Sheffield."

"Between Sir John and — one of the company?"

"One of the company, yes!"

"Man or woman?"

"Man!"

"Well — his name, Mr. Carroll?"

"This is very unpleasant," said Carroll. "Am I obliged — "

"You can tell it to me now, or you can tell it at the Coroner's inquest, within the next forty-eight hours, Mr. Carroll, whichever you like," replied Marston. "It's bound to come out! Better tell me, and be done with it."

"Well, it was with Mr. Macdermott. He has been a member — an important member of the company for the past three or four years, and lately the relations between him and Sir John have become strained."

"For what reason?"

"If I am to tell you the truth, Macdermott has of late given way to drink. My private belief is that he has some secret trouble. But he is a proud, gloomy, intensely reserved man, and will give his confidence to no one. Lately he has been drinking very hard, and last week, at Sheffield, he was unable to play his part one night. The next day Sir John had him in his room, and there was a violent scene in which hard words were used on both sides: I have an idea that Macdermott thinks he has a grievance against Sir John. Anyway, Sir John ordered me to give Macdermott his notice."

"Did you carry out his orders?"

"I had no option. If Sir John gave an order — to anyone — it had to be carried out, there and then. I have already told you — he was a martinet."

"Have you seen Macdermott tonight, Mr. Carroll?"

"I saw him when I assembled the company after hearing of Sir John's death. But I had heard something about him before that. I suppose, now that his name has come up, that I may as well tell you everything?"

"By all means! Don't keep anything back."

"Well, just before we heard the news, Mr. Gresford and I were talking near the box office. Ridsdale, another member of the company, came round to me there from the dressing rooms. He said that it was now approaching seven o'clock — it was five minutes to, as a matter of fact — and Macdermott hadn't come, and what was more, he, Ridsdale, didn't believe he was coming. He had seen Macdermott, he said, drinking with some townsmen in a bar of one of the town hotels at half-past five, and from something that Macdermott had said, Ridsdale had got the idea that he wasn't coming to his work. I was just going off to tell this to Sir John when the news of what had happened in the dressing room was brought to Mr. Gresford and myself."

"But you say Macdermott did come to the theatre — that he was present when you assembled the company?"

"Yes — he was there then. He had evidently come in after Ridsdale had been to me in the foyer."

"Was he dressed for his part?"

"No — he was in his own clothes. He had changed nothing."

"Did you speak to him?"

"No. I spoke to the company, generally."

"Did you observe him at all?"

"Yes, I did that. I could see quite well that he had been drinking."

"Did he show any particular emotion on hearing of the murder?"

"No! He was the only one of the company who didn't. The news I gave them affected the various members in various ways, as you will understand. Macdermott simply stared, fixedly, stolidly, at me until I'd finished what I had to say: he never moved a muscle of his face. When I'd finished he put his hat on and walked away."

"Is he still in the theatre?"

Gresford interposed.

"Jenkinson can tell us that," he said. "That is, if Macdermott left in the usual way."

He opened the door and called the doorkeeper. "Jenkinson," he said. "You know Mr. Macdermott — have you seen him leave?"

"Yes, sir," replied Jenkinson. "Mr. Macdermott went out, by himself, just before Mr. Marston and the other gentlemen came in."

"Where can we find him?" asked Marston. "Lodgings, I mean?"

"Jenkinson will know that, too," said Gresford. "Where's Mr. Macdermott lodging, Jenkinson?"

"Mrs. Smith, 35, Thornholme Street, sir," replied Jenkinson promptly. "Second street on the right from here. Mr. Macdermott's lodged there often, sir — this isn't his first visit to this theatre, you know, Mr. Gresford, though it was his first with Sir John Riversley. Mr. Macdermott, sir, has often played here in the old days."

Marston turned to Gresford as the doorkeeper retired.

"We may take it that Macdermott knows this theatre well, then?" he said. "By the by, what aged man is he?"

"About forty-five," replied Carroll.

Marston beckoned to Stell, who, from a quiet corner, had listened silently to all that had been said.

"Come with me, Stell," he said. "We'll go round to Thornholme Street. Wardle," he went on, drawing the Alderman aside, "do me a favour. Jump into a taxi; go down to the police station and tell the sergeant in charge to send me a couple of thoroughly dependable plainclothes men up to Thornholme Street at once. Let them wait at the corner till I speak to them."

He beckoned to the detective, and together they went out, and, through the crowds still lingering about the theatre, into the main street.

"Second on the right, eh?" he said. "I don't know Thornholme Street, I think."

"Theatrical lodgings street," said Stell. "Nearly every house — it's convenient for the theatre, you see."

"I wonder if we shall find this chap in?" remarked Marston. "What do you think of it, Stell?"

"He'd only a quarter of an hour to do it in — as far as I can make out," replied Stell.

"You can do a lot in that way in a quarter of an hour — if you mean to do it!" said Marston. "But that's what I'll ask him to tell me — where was he between six-thirty and six-forty-five? Easy to answer — if he will. Here's the house — Number thirty-five."

A moment later, ushered by a wondering landlady, the two men walked into a parlour liberally decorated with the signed photographs of theatrical celebrities, to find Macdermott, a good-looking man spoilt by the marks of obvious dissipation, seated before a bright fire, pipe in mouth and bottle and glass at his elbow. He had a book in his hand, and he retained it as he rose and looked questioningly at his visitors. But he did not speak.

"Mr. Macdermott," said Marston, going straight to the point, "I am the Chief Constable of this place. I have just come from the Theatre Royal, where, as you know, Sir John Riversley was murdered this evening. I have had some information given me which affects yourself. You won't mind my asking you a plain question in plain words? Your answer will save you and me a lot of trouble. Where were you, Mr. Macdermott, between six-thirty and six-forty-five tonight? Will you say, please?"

Macdermott drew himself up and looked straight back at his questioner.

"No, sir!" he said firmly. "No, sir, I will not say!"

Chapter 3

GO BACK!

THERE was something so uncompromising and even truculent about the actor's tone and demeanour that Marston for the moment was completely taken aback. But at the end of that moment he returned to the charge.

"Mr. Macdermott!" he said sternly. "Let me advise you not to be foolish! This is a case of murder. And to be plain with you, I have good reason for asking an answer to my question. What harm can it do you to reply to it? It's simple. I'm only asking you to say where you were between six-thirty and six-forty-five this evening."

Macdermott flung his book down on the table between them. It was as if he flung down a gage of defiance.

"I will not say, sir! — my business, and mine alone!" he replied. "But I'll tell you where I wasn't. I wasn't in or about the Hatherford Theatre Royal!"

"In that case, Mr. Macdermott, why not say where you were? It need go no further."

"No, sir — I say nothing. Why should I? As I said — my business. Not yours, nor anybody else's."

"I'll tell you why, Mr. Macdermott — you see, I'm being frank with you. We've heard something — information supplied, you know. You've been on bad terms with Sir John Riversley for the past few days. A quarrel."

Macdermott shrugged his shoulders.

"Jack Riversley and I have had many a quarrel," he said sneeringly. "This was probably the twentieth. There was nothing in it."

"You were under notice," said Marston.

"I've been under notice half a dozen times! The notice would have been withdrawn before Saturday. Jack Riversley couldn't do without me."

He said that with a laugh, and picking up his book, dropped back into the easy chair. But the next instant he was on his legs again, making for a sideboard, whereon stood a range of tumblers and wine glasses, flanked by various bottles.

"Forgetting myself," he said with another laugh. "What'll you drink, gentlemen? And these," he went on, pointing to an open box of cigars, "are good. Try them!"

"Nothing, thank you," said Marston. He was still taken aback by the man's cool and aggressive demeanour. "Come, Mr. Macdermott!" he went on. "Just think now! — this is, or may be, more serious than you apparently reckon it to be. You say you weren't in or about the Theatre Royal between six-thirty and six-forty-five. I don't know what you mean by that word 'about'? You must have been somewhere about; for you were there soon after six-forty-five — I mean, you were seen there in the dressing rooms soon after six-forty-five. Carroll, your business manager — "

"Carroll is a damned skunk!" interrupted Macdermott. "A mischief-maker!"

"Mischief-maker or not, he's speaking the truth there," said Marston. "You were there at the time I mention!"

"But not between half-past six and a quarter to seven!" retorted Macdermott. "For during that quarter of an hour and the quarter of an hour preceding it, I was — elsewhere!"

"It must have been close by, then — "

"I never said it wasn't, did I? Have it at that, if you like. Close by!"

Once more Marston felt himself baffled. But he persisted.

"Will you tell me when you last saw Sir John Riversley?" he asked.

"Will I tell you when I last saw Jack Riversley? With pleasure! I last saw Jack Riversley as we left the stage together on Saturday night at Sheffield. I've never set eyes on him since, alive or dead!"

"You didn't travel here with him?"

"Travel here with him? My good sir, do you think Jack Riversley would so far forget himself as to travel with his company? We poor beggars, my good sir, travel third class; Jack Riversley travelled in his own Rolls Royce car — which is no doubt garaged at his hotel. Pshaw!"

Marston gave the actor a long and steady look.

"There was bad feeling between you and Sir John Riversley, Mr. Macdermott," he remarked. "I can judge that — by your tone."

"Bad feeling? Not on my part. Differences, yes! Quarrels, yes! He's gone now, however, and — you know the old Latin tag? — *de mortuis nil nisi bonum*. I'm not going to say any more about him: I have my own private opinion of him, based on an intimate acquaintanceship of twenty years. I have nothing more to say, gentlemen. Except this — I wish to be left alone, with my pipe, my glass, my book. Allow me to ring for my landlady."

"A moment " said Marston. "You won't say where you were between six-thirty and six-forty-five — on reflection?"

"I will not! — and shall not, if I reflect all night, which I shan't! I will say nothing — either to you, or before the Coroner who will doubtless hold his enquiry, or before a magistrate, or before a judge and jury. But I will say this, Mr. Chief Constable! If you want to get at the secret of Jack Riversley's murder, for he was murdered, and his murderer made no mistake about it, either — if, I say, you want to solve the mystery, go back twenty-two or -three years! Jack Riversley was born in this town of

Hatherford; he lived here till he was two- or three-and-twenty; he left secrets behind him. Find them out! Gentlemen, you will now excuse me!"

He turned and rang the bell; a moment later, and Marston and Stell found themselves outside the house.

"What do you think of that, Stell?" asked the Chief Constable. "Cool hand! Is it all bluff?"

Stell walked some distance along the street before he replied.

"I'll tell you what I do think," he said after a pause — "I think there may be a good deal in what he said last. Go back!"

"To Sir John's early days, eh?" asked Marston.

"Just that! He may have had enemies — an enemy — a particular enemy — in the town."

"Possible! You're not a Yorkshireman, Stell?"

"Londoner!"

"Well, I'm a Surrey man. You know what they say about these Yorkshiremen? That a Yorkshireman will carry a stone in his pocket for ten years, and at the end of ten years he'll turn it over in his pocket — but he'll fling it in the end, whether he keeps it ten years or twenty? And it's true — from what I've seen of 'em! So — "

"So there may be something in what Macdermott suggested," said Stell. "The thing is — to find it out."

Marston paused, pointing to the end of the street.

"There are our two men," he said. "Wardle's lost no time. Now look here, before we go up to them, what do you advise next? You're a smart chap, Stell; you've done two or three big things, and here's another big thing. I'm going to leave this case in your hands. What do you suggest next? What do you want to do?"

"I've thought that out, while we were with Macdermott," replied Stell. "I want to go down to the Midland Hotel and find out everything I can about Sir John's movements since his arrival here yesterday."

"Good! That's practical. Of course, we know something. He lunched today at the City Hall, with the Mayor and a few prominent townsmen. I was there; so was Alderman Wardle and Dr. Grayle. Sir John made a speech — short — in which he referred to his connection with the town. Nothing in it, though — nothing, I mean, that can help us, at present. Yes, that's a good notion of yours. Go down there and get to know all you can. Then come and tell me. Now let's deal with these two men," concluded Marston, as they reached the corner. "Who are they? — oh, Robertshaw and Morgan — they're all right."

The two plainclothes men, lounging near a lamppost, stood to attention as the Chief Constable came up.

"Now, my lads," said Marston, "here's a job for you that requires care and watchfulness. There's a man in this street who's got to be kept under strict observation. An actor, named Macdermott. Do either of you know him by sight? He's played here before, but it's some time ago."

"I know him, sir," replied the elder of the two. "Seen him several times. Used to come here with the Mossford Company."

"Well, he's at number thirty-five. Keep a strict watch on the house. If he goes out tonight, follow him. Keep a watch on the house all night, and tomorrow morning too — you can arrange matters between yourselves. If he makes any movement, let me know at once. That's all."

He turned away with Stell, crossing the road towards the theatre, around which a crowd was still gathered.

"Well, off you go, Stell, to the Midland," he said. "I'll rejoin the doctors. Come to my office with whatever news you get. There'll not be much going to bed tonight, I reckon! Anyway, you'll find me at the City Hall, whatever time it is."

Stell nodded, and turning away to his right, made for the centre of the town. Presently he stopped, took a cigarette case from his vest pocket, and lighting a cigarette, began to smoke. And after a puff or two, and as he walked on again, he spoke aloud.

"It wasn't that chap!" he said softly. "I watched him! Who, then?"

Five minutes walk brought him to the Midland Hotel — a palatial building fronting the main square of the place. The entrance hall and the lounge were packed with people — men and women: Stell felt that they were discussing the tragedy. As he passed through on his way to the office two or three men hailed him; Stell gave them no more attention than to nod; he was not going to gossip. Presently he was with the manager in a private room.

"You've heard what's taken place at the theatre?" said Stell.

"We've heard — yes! Awful! They telephoned. But we know no details. Was it — murder?"

"Murder, without doubt. Nothing less! Deliberate."

"Anybody taken? Suspected?"

"Never mind that — can't say yet. I want some information from you. Sir John had a suite of rooms here?"

"Yes."

"When did he get here?"

"Well, he himself came in about five o'clock yesterday afternoon, Sunday. His chauffeur came with the car and luggage about three."

"Two hours before Sir John?"

"Just so!"

"Did the chauffeur say where Sir John was?"

"He didn't. He only said he'd be along during the afternoon."

"What did Sir John do after he got here?"

"Well, he didn't go out of his rooms till after he'd dined — he dined in his private sitting room at seven. About eight o'clock last night he went out, on foot. He came back about half-past ten."

"What about today?"

"Well, his business manager, Mr. Carroll, came to see him about ten o'clock this morning. He was with him an hour or so. Then the Mayor came — he'd a gentleman with him whom I knew well enough by sight, through seeing him frequently about the town, but I don't know his name. Sir John's dresser looked in, too. About one o'clock a reporter from the Hatherford Observer called; he was with Sir John about ten minutes. Then, soon after one, Sir John went to the City Hall — he spoke to me as he went out and said he was going to lunch with the Mayor and a few friends."

"Do you know what time he came in again?"

"Yes. Two or three people called on him in the afternoon — this afternoon, of course. Big pots in the town, you know. Lady Smith-Robinson was one; Sir Charles Popham another. Sir John wasn't in. He didn't come in till half-past five. Then he had what these actors always have — a sort of high tea: fish, eggs, and so on. He went off to the theatre about twenty past six; he looked in at the office as he went out, and gave me a half-sheet of notepaper to give to the head waiter; he'd written down on it what he wanted for supper at half-past eleven, and he mentioned that it was to be for two; a friend would come in with him."

"Say who the friend was?"

"No!"

"And that was the last you saw of him?"

"The last!"

Stell had been making notes of all this: he looked up from his notebook. "Is that chauffeur of Sir John's anywhere about?" he asked. "He is? Fetch him."

The manager returned with the chauffeur in a few minutes — Stell looked him over.

"You drove your master here from Sheffield yesterday?" he said. "Did you stop anywhere on the way?"

"Not till we got nearly into Hatherford," replied the chauffeur. "We did, then."

"Where?"

"I don't know Hatherford. It was about a mile from the middle of the town, on the Weatherfield Road. Working-class, rather low district. Sir John pulled me up, got out, and said he'd walk the rest of the way: I was to go on to this hotel. I did so."

"What time was that — when you left him?"

"That," said the chauffeur, "would be about ten minutes to three o'clock."

Chapter 4

FLIGHT

AT that moment the telephone on the manager's desk rang out sharply. He picked up the receiver.

"Hullo?"

"Is that the Midland Hotel? This is Marston, Chief Constable. Is Stell there? Yes? Tell him to come to me at once at the Theatre Royal. Urgent!"

Stell slipped his notebook into his pocket and went off without a word. He ran all the way to the theatre and went straight along the passage from the stage door to the dressing room in which Sir John Riversley had been found dead; he knew somehow that Marston would be there. And there Marston was, with Gresford, and Carroll, and Pratt, the dresser, and two theatre employees whom Stell did not know. But the dead man was there no longer, nor the two doctors.

Marston took Stell aside.

"Learned anything down there?" he asked.

"Certain things," replied Stell. "They need enquiring into. One is — Sir John Riversley's movements here in the town between three and five o'clock yesterday, Sunday, afternoon: the other, his movements this afternoon, from the time he left the Mayor's luncheon party to the time he returned to the hotel.

There's some mystery about his doings yesterday afternoon, anyhow — and may be about his doings today."

"We'll go into that later," said Marston. "But listen — I've got new evidence here about Macdermott. Those two men over there — one's the gas man; the other's the carpenter. They saw Macdermott coming away from this room!"

"After the murder?"

"You shall hear what they say. Here, Thorp — just tell Mr. Stell what you've told me — about seeing Mr. Macdermott tonight."

The gas man came forward.

"Why, sir, there's not much to tell," he said. "Just what I told you, of course. I did see Mr. Macdermott — and that's about all."

"We'd better show Mr. Stell where you saw him," said Marston. "Come this way, Stell." He opened one of the three doors which gave access to the room and revealed a narrow passage, lighted in the middle by a single lamp. Thorp, motioned to lead the way, turned to the left, and going in front came to a square lobby, on one side of which was the opening of a flight of stairs. He pointed to this.

"He was there when we saw him, sir — me and Simpson," he said. "Leastways, we saw him come out of this passage and go up the stairs."

"Where were you?" asked Stell.

Thorp pointed to a door on the other side of the lobby.

"Simpson and me were just within that doorway, Mr. Stell," he answered. "We keep things — tools and so on — in there. The door was open."

"Did Macdermott see you?"

"I don't think he did. He didn't look at us, anyway, nor speak to us, as he would have done if he'd seen us — we both know him well, you know; he's played here before, years ago. No, I'm sure he didn't see us. He just came out of this end of the passage and went up those stairs. He was looking down — as if he was in a brown study."

"Where do these stairs lead to?" enquired Stell.

"Dressing rooms — next floor."

Stell turned to the carpenter who, at Marston's signal, had followed them.

"You see this, too, Simpson?" he asked.

"I saw just what Thorp saw," replied Simpson. "Just! Macdermott came along the passage and went up the stairs. That's all."

Stell turned and went back along the passage. Beyond the door opening into the room in which Sir John Riversley's dead body had been found was another door, closing the end of the passage. Stell pointed to it.

"What's that door open on?" he asked.

"The street, sir — side street," replied Simpson. "It's really the manager's private entrance."

"Is it open — I mean, could anybody come in that way — anybody who happened to try it from outside?" asked Stell.

"Can't say, sir — Mr. Gresford has a latchkey for it, but — "

Stell walked forward and tried the door. It opened at his touch and for a second he looked out on the street at the side of the theatre. Then he called Gresford from the dressing room.

"This door — your private door — is open," he said. "Did you know?"

"I usually leave it open," replied Gresford. "It's convenient. Sir John could have come in by it if he'd known of it — I meant to show it to him. You see, he'd never been here before."

"Do you think Macdermott knew of it?"

"He may have done; he's played here several times, you know. Years ago — he knows this theatre well."

Stell drew Marston aside.

"I don't think there's anything in this," he said. "Macdermott told us that we could take it that between six-thirty and six-forty-five he was close by the theatre. My opinion is that knowing of this private door, he tried it, found it open, and entered by it, then went straight along the passage and upstairs to his dressing room. There's nothing to show he entered Sir John's room."

Marston gave him a significant look.

"Isn't there?" he said. "Look at this, then!"

He drew from his pocket a small packet wrapped in thin paper, and from this extracted a white cambric pocket handkerchief, part of which bore the marks of burning. On what remained there were two or three obvious bloodstains.

"I found this myself," said Marston. "After the body had been removed, I made a careful inspection of the room. I found this handkerchief thrown in the grate; whoever had thrown it there had not been sufficiently careful to see that it went into the open fire. As a matter of fact, it had fallen on the hob at the side of the fire, and while a good deal of it had caught and was charred, all this was left intact. Now look at the corner. There are two initials, worked in red — you see what they are. M.M. Macdermott's christian name is Michael! What do you think of that, Stell?"

Stell took the fragment of handkerchief and examined it.

"That's blood!" he said. "And the initials are as you say. But I can't conceive any man being so utterly careless and foolish as to — " "As not to see that the thing was burned!" interrupted Marston. "Aye, but he was in a hurry! And — they always make some mistake. This was Macdermott's mistake. If he'd put this thing right into the fire — but he didn't. Stell! — there's no doubt about it, to my thinking! Still, there's a thing I'll point out to you. Come into the dressing room again."

He led the way back to the dressing room; Gresford and Carroll were there in one corner, talking in whispers; Pratt was there, too, still lachrymose. Marston led Stell to the dressing table on which traces of the tragedy were still apparent.

"Look here!" he said. "Nothing's been touched. You see how things were laid out for Sir John's make up? Now, do you see that? — a small pile of clean pocket handkerchiefs. Pratt tells me that that was one of Sir John's peculiarities — he liked a supply of these things to be placed on his table every night, or whenever he was performing. Put here, do you see, so that he could pick up a clean one whenever he liked. Pratt tells me, too, that he came to the theatre — Pratt, I mean — at four-thirty this afternoon, and laid out all Sir John's things in readiness for his coming at six-thirty; when he'd done that, Pratt went to his lodgings to get his tea. Now, we'll ask Pratt a question. Pratt, come here! You laid out these handkerchiefs at the corner of the table, as usual?"

"Yes, sir — just where you see them," replied Pratt.

"Can you be positively certain how many you laid out?"

"Yes, sir — positive. Because I always lay out the same number every time."

"Well, how many, then?"

"Half a dozen, sir."

Marston turned the handkerchiefs over, counting them.

"There are five here!" he said. "Now then, did the murderer take off the top one, the sixth? If he did, and if it's the one I found half-burned, how came a handkerchief of Macdermott's amongst handkerchiefs of Sir John's?"

"Mixed up in the same laundry," said Stell.

"Maybe! But if Macdermott had known that it was his handkerchief that he picked up from this pile he wouldn't have picked it up! He thought it was — one of Sir John's. He never noticed his own initials on it. Coincidence, you say? Is there such a thing? Stell! — we've got to take Macdermott!"

Stell said nothing for a minute or two. Marston watched him. He had a very high opinion of Stell's abilities, but he was secretly wondering why Stell seemed doubtful. To himself the case was clear; he had a profound belief in the obvious.

"Macdermott's safe — with those two men keeping an eye on the house," said Stell at last. "And as I told you, there's a good deal of mystery surrounding Sir John Riversley's movements since he came here yesterday. Still — there'd be no harm in seeing Macdermott again and asking him for further explanations."

"You don't think he did it, Stell?" said Marston.

"Well, if you put it that way, frankly I don't! I never have done," replied Stell. "I won't say he doesn't know something, though. But I don't attach any importance to the fact of his having entered the theatre by that private door, nor any to your finding of this handkerchief with his initials — I should say that the handkerchief got mixed up with Sir John Riversley's, at some laundry. Probably, as they were constantly touring together, their things went to the same laundry in some town or other. No — I want to turn my attention to the doings of Sir John himself, after he got here yesterday. But, as I say, there'd be no harm in seeing Macdermott again and asking him a question or two."

"Come on, then; we'll go back to Thornholme Street," said Marston. "And after we've seen him, I'll decide what to do."

He said a word or two to Gresford and Carroll, and went out, followed by Stell; together they made their way through the crowd that still lingered about the theatre, in dwindling numbers, and went along to Thornholme Street. Opposite number thirty-five they found Robertshaw and Morgan.

"Anything happened?" asked Marston.

"Nothing!" replied Robertshaw.

"Nobody come out?"

"Nobody's come out, or gone in, since you were here, sir," said Morgan.

"Well, stay where you are — I may want you," remarked Marston. "We're going to make a call there."

He crossed the road and rang the bell of number thirty-five: Stell touched his elbow, pointing to the front window of the lower storey.

"No light in the room in which we saw him!" he said.

"Gone to bed, perhaps," answered Marston.

"It isn't nine o'clock, yet," replied Stell.

The door opened: Mrs. Smith appeared.

"Mr. Macdermott in?" asked Marston, stepping inside. "I want to see him again."

The landlady drew back, shaking her head.

"Mr. Macdermott's gone, sir!" she said. "He went out just after you'd called."

"Gone?" exclaimed Marston. "He — here, let us come in, Mrs. Smith. That room, if you please — turn the light on. Now," he went on, as the landlady preceded them into the sitting room in which they had interviewed Macdermott, "tell me — all about it, quick!"

"Why, sir, I don't know that there's much to tell," said the landlady. "It's no concern of mine, you know, sir. As soon as you'd gone, Mr. Macdermott went upstairs. He was down again in a very few minutes. He'd his overcoat on, and his suitcase — he'd only one — was on that table. 'Mrs. Smith,' he said, 'you know what's happened tonight? — Sir John Riversley's been murdered in his dressing room. Those two men who came just now were police officers; they wanted information from me. I've none to give them,' he said, 'I know nothing at all about the murder — nothing. And I don't want to be, and won't be, mixed up with it, and as there'll be no performances, I'm going. Tell me what I owe you, and I'll be off.' Well, sir, I told him, and he paid me, and he went away, then and there. He was off within — well, I should say a quarter of an hour of your being here, sir."

"How did he go?" asked Marston. "Cab?"

"No, sir. He went out of my back door — into Halfpenny Passage, at the back of the house. That leads down into Station Street, sir."

"Give any reason for going that way, Mrs. Smith?"

"No, sir — he'd gone in and out that way two or three times since he came here on Sunday afternoon. It's convenient."

"You didn't hear him say that he thought he was being watched?"

"Oh, no, sir! He said just what I've told you — word for word. And, oh, yes, there was just one more thing he said as he was going out. A message for you, sir. 'If that Chief Constable calls here again, Mrs. Smith,' he said, tell him that he'll hear from me, in due course.' His very words, sir!"

A few minutes later Marston and Stell were out in the street again.

"That's pretty good, Stell!" said the Chief Constable. "It is, indeed! I shall hear from him — in due course! Well, of all the — "

Chapter 5

LOOKING BACK

THERE were three principal railway stations in Hatherford — termini — to say nothing of some twelve or fifteen smaller ones, and there was an important junction five miles outside the city; there were also tram and bus facilities in plenty: Marston realised that to institute a search there and then for a man who had had a good, full hour's start would be so much waste of time. Blaming himself for forgetting that Mrs. Smith probably had a back door to her house, he dismissed the two plainclothes men and returned with Stell to the theatre. There he sought out Carroll.

"Macdermott's gone!" he said. "He sneaked off from his lodgings just after we'd called on him. I'm not going to say anything as to whether that's suspicious or not; he's evidently a queer fellow. But I want some further information about him from you, Mr. Carroll. First, do you know if he has any permanent address?"

Carroll looked doubtful.

"I believe — that is, I've an idea that he has a sort of pied-a-terre in town," he answered. "Somewhere up Maida Vale way. But I don't know exactly where it is. Portsdown Road, I fancy. Some of the company may know, but they've all gone now. I can enquire for you."

"Do!" said Marston. "Find out, if you can, and let me know at my office. Now the second question. Do you know anything of Macdermott's private affairs? Has he any means beyond what he earns? What I'm trying to get at is this — is he likely to have money on him, or have money easily obtainable?"

"Macdermott's not without money," replied Carroll. "He's a very queer chap — drink is his failing — but he's keen about money. I know he has money. For one thing he's a half share in at least two highly successful plays — melodramas — now running in the provinces: for another, I also know that he's a certain amount of money of his own. Oh, yes, you can take it that he's not short of money."

"Get out of this country, if he wanted, eh?" suggested Marston.

"I daresay. But I don't think he will. If I may say so, I think you're wrong if you think Macdermott had anything to do with Sir John's death. Macdermott's a man of very irascible, and even violent temper, but in his worst and ugliest moods he's always a substratum of common sense about him. If I may so put it, his weapon is his tongue. I've seen him in quarrels and altercations — he's a fiend at such times, but it's all in words. I've never seen him lift a finger — but I've seen him goad other men to such fury that they were fit to murder him!"

"Well . . . ," said Marston. He paused, as if reflecting on the business manager's last words. "There isn't any other member of your company that you suspect at all — is there?"

Carroll looked surprised.

"Good Heavens, no!" he answered. "None!"

Marston motioned Stell to follow him and left the theatre. He hailed a passing taxicab, and they went down to the City Hall. Wardle was just coming down the steps at the entrance to the police headquarters. He paused.

"Well? — anything new?" he asked.

"Come back to my office," said Marston. "We'll talk. What time is it? — twenty past nine. Time to do a lot yet. This is how matters stand," he went on when the three had reached his room and were alone there. "We've got certain additional evidence — I consider it evidence — which seems to incriminate Macdermott, and Macdermott has taken his departure! He made off as soon as Stell and I had left him. And as I hear that he's a sort of chap who always has plenty of ready money about him, and as I'm sure he's a keen-witted fellow, in spite of his failing in the drink way, I reckon we shall have a job to find him. However, let's hear what you've got to say now, Stell. You got some information at the Midland Hotel, you say — let's have it."

"I think there are queer features about it," said Stell. "I got little from the manager; just certain plain facts that one would expect to get. But I saw Sir John's chauffeur. Now listen! This chap drove Sir John from Sheffield to Hatherford yesterday — Sunday. They didn't stop anywhere — it's only forty miles or so — till they got to a little way outside the town here. The chauffeur says he doesn't know Hatherford, but from what he told me, I judge that Sir John pulled him up in the Marradale district — it was, said the chauffeur, about a mile from the town, on the Weatherfield Road. That would be in Marradale — "

Wardle let out an inarticulate exclamation.

"What is it?" asked Marston.

"Never mind — just now!" replied Wardle. "Tell you afterwards. Let Stell finish."

"Well," continued Stell. "As I say, Sir John pulled him up there, got out of the car, told him he'd walk the rest of the way into the town, and bade him go on with the car and the luggage to the Midland Hotel, where they were expected. The chauffeur did so. According to him, it was just about ten minutes to three o'clock when he set Sir John down in Marradale. Sir John turned up at the hotel, on foot, about five o'clock. Now then, what I want to know is this. What was he doing during those two hours? Where did he go? Did he call on anybody? If so, who was it? There's an element of mystery in this business! Why did he get out there at all? That's a poor working-class quarter — about the poorest in the city: a good deal of it's practically slum."

Wardle smote his fist on the desk by which he was sitting.

"But it wasn't always a slum, my lad, nor a poor working-class quarter, either!" he exclaimed. "I know why Sir John Riversley stopped his car there! He wanted to see his old house! His father and mother — aye, and his father's father and grandfather before him — lived in Marradale Hall, that fine old stone house that's now falling into ruins — more shame to our Corporation for letting it! That's what he was after — wanted to see the old place — his birthplace. Simple!"

"Would it take him two hours to do that?" asked Stell.

"Why, he may have talked to some of the people thereabouts," replied Wardle. "You'd better go up there tomorrow morning and make enquiries. Of course, I see nothing mysterious in this, Stell. Natural thing for a man, coming back to the place of his birth, to want to see the old spot."

"What about this afternoon, Stell?" asked Marston.

"I haven't gone into that, of course, but I'm going to," replied the detective. "I want to know where Sir John Riversley was, what he did, whom he saw, who saw or spoke with him, between the time he left the Mayor's luncheon party and the time he returned to the Midland Hotel. And when that's done, I want a good deal more. That man Macdermott, whatever he may be, spoke commonsense when he said 'Go back!' I want to know all about Sir John Riversley's previous connection with Hatherford — when he was a young man."

"I know a man who can give you all that," remarked Wardle. "That's old Mr. Atley. He was a close friend of Sir John's father — in fact, he was at one time his partner. Mr. Atley's as well acquainted with the history of that family as anybody in the town, and although he's ageing, his memory's as good as mine — better, on some points. Those old chaps can always remember things of the past better than things of the present."

"Where does Mr. Atley live?" asked Stell.

"Mr. Atley lives up Worton way — Ashgrove," replied Wardle. "Near me. But" — he pulled out his watch — "I know where I can lay hands on him just now. He's always — he's a widower — he's always at the Conservative Club, right opposite where we're sitting, till ten o'clock every night — at ten, punctually, he goes home. I'll step across and fetch him, if you like."

He left the room without waiting for an answer, and Marston looked enquiringly at Stell.

"What's your notion, Stell?" he asked.

"I think Sir John may have had an enemy here," replied Stell. "You know what you said about a Yorkshireman carrying a stone for ten years? There may be somebody in this town who's cherished a what-you-might-call-lifelong hatred of Sir John and who waited for an opportunity to have revenge. And I can't forget this. There must be no end of people — men — regular theatregoers — who are perfectly familiar with the ins-and-outs of the Theatre Royal, and know all about that private door! Just look how easy it would be for anybody to enter by that door, dodge into the dressing room which Sir John occupied, and dodge out again. And Gresford admitted that the door was open."

"You dismiss Macdermott, then?" asked Marston.

"I never suspected Macdermott," said Stell. "One has an instinct — an intuition — in these things."

"All the same, he's got to be found," declared Marston. "I'm not going to let any man give me the slip like that! And there are questions that he'll have to answer at the inquest."

Wardle came back just then, accompanied by a little, rosy-cheeked gentleman, who plainly showed his surprise at his surroundings.

"Mr. Atley," said Wardle.

"Take this chair, Mr. Atley," said Marston, drawing forward the one easy chair in the place. "Much obliged to you, sir, for coming over. Interests of justice, you know, Mr. Atley."

Mr. Atley sat down, smiled, and looked about him — and particularly at a case of burglars' tools which hung over Marston's mantelpiece.

"Why," he said cheerily, "I don't know that I can tell you very much, Mr. Chief Constable. Alderman Wardle says you want to know what I know about the Riversley family: terribly sad thing this is, about young John — of course, I remember him being born! His father, another John, and I were partners at that time; we dissolved partnership some ten years later. Oh, yes, I knew the family well enough. They lived, till Sir John's father died, some fifteen years ago — the mother had died before that — at Marradale Hall, which is now let off in tenements, and a great shame, too — the Corporation ought to have bought that old house and made it into a museum."

"You knew Sir John Riversley as a young man, Mr. Atley?" asked Marston.

"Aye, and as a boy, too — knew him from his birth till the time he left the town," replied Mr. Atley. "He would be twenty-two, or, perhaps, twenty-three when he left Hatherford and went, definitely, on the stage. Except that he came to his mother's, and afterwards, to his father's funeral, I don't think he's ever been in the town since — till now. And now — "

"Mr. Atley!" said Marston as the old gentleman paused, shaking his head. "What sort of a character had Sir John in those days? What sort of a young man was he?"

"Well, I can't say that he didn't give his father and mother a good deal of anxiety," replied Mr. Atley. "For he did! Not as much as some young men do, to be sure, but still sufficient to trouble them a good deal. Drink? No! — never remember hearing that of him — my recollection of him as a young man is that he was exceedingly temperate. But he'd two failings. One was — gambling!"

"Horseracing?" suggested Marston.

"That was one form. He got mixed up with a man who was a well-known bookmaker in the town in those days — he's dead now. The other was cards. His father had to make good for him more than once over cards and horses. He'd — I don't know if he kept it up in later life — but he'd the tastes and instincts of a born gambler."

"His business manager, Mr. Carroll, tells me that in his experience of him Sir John was a keen businessman who knew the value of money," observed Marston. "He'd the reputation, too, of being a bit tough with his employees."

"Very likely — he'd no doubt altered his views," said Mr. Atley. "I'm telling you what he was as a young man. No doubt he learnt wisdom by experience. He certainly had that vice when he was young — I remember how it troubled his father. But he'd another — he was too fond of the ladies."

"Ah!" exclaimed Marston. "The ladies, eh?"

"Well," continued Mr. Atley, with an indulgent smile. "You know what a very striking and handsome man he was, poor fellow! But handsome as he was in middle age, it was nothing to his handsomeness as a young man. And you know from the time he was eighteen he was a prominent member of the Hatherford Amateur Dramatic Society. There were a great many ladies in it — wives, daughters, sisters, of prominent townsmen — and I daresay the young fellow was flattered a good deal, and made up to a good deal — he was just the sort to attract, and no doubt his head got turned."

"Any scandals?" asked Stell, abruptly.

Mr. Atley hesitated.

"All between ourselves, sir," said Stell.

"Oh, well, there was one," replied the old gentleman. "But I'm not going to give you any names, for though the lady is dead, her husband's alive. You see, the Society was playing the 'Lady of Lyons' one winter, and young Riversley, of course, played Claude Melnotte. The Pauline was a very pretty — and very impressionable — young married woman. Her husband got jealous — thought he'd cause for his jealousy — there was a row — trouble. It came to an end by young Riversley leaving the town. Keep that to yourselves — the husband is still alive."

"You'll give me his name — if need be?" asked Stell. "If it's absolutely necessary?"

"Well," said Mr. Atley, unwillingly, "if it is absolutely necessary."

Presently he and Wardle went away together, and Stell resumed his hat and overcoat.

"Where are you off, now, Stell?" asked Marston.

"Hatherford Observer office," replied Stell. "I want some press help now."

Chapter 6

THE STRANGE GENTLEMAN

THE Hatherford Observer came out next morning with a full account of the tragedy of the preceding evening, supplemented with a sketch of the dead man's career, and ornamented by several photographs of him in mufti and in character. Stell paid little attention to all this; the only paragraph which interested him was one in big type which he himself had dictated to a sympathetic sub-editor. Would anyone who had seen Sir John Riversley anywhere in Hatherford between three and five o'clock on Sunday afternoon or between the same hours on Monday afternoon communicate with the police authorities at once? In Stell's reckoning there ought to have been a prompt result of that appeal: it seemed an utter impossibility that a noticeable man like Sir John Riversley could have escaped observation. But by two o'clock that Tuesday afternoon, when the Coroner opened his enquiry, there had been no result; nobody had come forward: Marston and Stell went to the inquest no wiser than they had been the night before. The opening of the inquest was a mere formal affair; within a quarter of an hour the Coroner, after supplementing Stell's request through the newspaper for information, had adjourned the proceedings for a fortnight, and the police went away to continue their investigations.

Stell was puzzled. As regards the two hours on Sunday afternoon, he figured things out in this way — Marradale, whatever it had been in the past, was now a working-class district of a rather poor sort; some of it was, as he had remarked, little better than a slum. How was it that a man of such handsome — and to say the least of it — distinguished presence as Sir John Riversley could escape notice there? On Sunday afternoon, when there was no work going, there would be no end of people about in the streets of Marradale — how was it no one had seen a man whose presence would certainly attract attention? Then again as regards Monday afternoon — Sir John had left the Mayor's parlour about three o'clock, and had been accompanied to the front entrance of the City Hall by two or three of his fellow guests. He had taken leave of them there and they had watched him cross the City Square and turn into Market Street. But from that moment until he turned up at his hotel, some two hours later, no trace of him could be had. This Monday disappearance puzzled Stell more than the affair of Sunday. Market Street was the main street of the city; at the time Sir John Riversley turned into it from the City Square it would be alive with people. Now Sir John's pictures were all over the town; photographs of him were in no end of shop windows — how came it that nobody had recognised him? If he had walked a hundred yards along Market Street he must have passed and been passed by hundreds of people. Why did no one come forward? Where had he gone when he turned the corner? True, at that corner was a cab rank — had he jumped into a cab and gone off in it somewhere? But Stell got no help there; he interviewed every cabman who had been on the rank that afternoon, none of them had seen Sir John. Nobody had seen him! — anyhow, nobody came forward to say he had.

"There's this much about it," remarked Wardle, discussing matters with Marston and Stell. "You've got to remember that ten yards or so past the corner of Market Street there's Weigh-House Passage. If he turned into that he'd be, in one minute, in one of the oldest and quietest quarters of the town — little frequented now, though, to be sure, it's a short cut from Market Street to Weatherfield Road. Probably he did turn into it. And if he once got into any working-class district, why should he be recognised? The folks would just think he was some well-to-do business man, up that way to look at a mill, or to call on some manufacturer — there was nothing unusual about his dress. I know how he was dressed at that luncheon party — just like any other well-dressed man. Morning coat, top hat, striped trousers — all very smart London West End cut, of course, but we've plenty of men in Hatherford just as smart. I think that's where he went — up Weatherfield Road again, to Marradale, where he sprang from. But why? And how is it nobody from that district comes forward? He must have spoken to somebody, surely."

Marston had a sudden idea.

"Where are his father and mother buried?" he asked. "One of the town cemeteries?"

"No! Happen to know that," replied Wardle. "They're buried at Hatherdale Church, fifteen miles away, family grave."

"Perhaps he took a cab and went out there, to see their graves?" suggested Marston. "There's something in that notion!"

But Stell shook his head.

"I should say that every cab driver in the place knows of our enquiries by this time," he said. "Not a man's come forward to say that he drove Sir John anywhere! Besides, why should he employ a taxi cab? He'd a car of his own, a Rolls Royce, at the Midland Garage."

Marston spread his hands.

"Well, there you are!" he said. "But he must have been somewhere, you know! We may hear something after the evening papers come out. You've got to remember, Stell, that the working folks — such as live up Marradale way — don't read the morning paper; they've no time. The evening paper's their purveyor of news. Have you seen to that?"

"I've seen to it," said Stell. "They're going to make a special feature of it in the five o'clock edition of the Evening Chronicle."

He went away then to pursue some further enquiries of his own, and a little later was leaving the City Hall when a policeman called after him.

"Chief wants you in his office," said the policeman. "At once!"

Stell went back to Marston's room; Wardle was there. Marston stood at his desk, holding a letter at which he was gazing with a frown on his face.

"Stell!" said Marston. "Here's a letter from that chap Macdermott! Came a few minutes ago by express post from London. I've just read it to Alderman Wardle. Here — read it for yourself. Talk about assurance! Or impudence!"

He tossed the letter over, and Stell sat down and read. There was no address on the letter, and no date.

MR. CHIEF CONSTABLE OF HATHERFORD, —

When I bade farewell to my landlady, Mrs. Smith, last night, I charged her with a message for yourself, which I have no doubt she has delivered to you. It was that you would hear from me in due course. I hasten — from my safe retreat — to discharge my promise.

After your visit to me last night I had no option but to leave Hatherford at once. Indeed, there was nothing left for me to do there. The death of Sir John Riversley put an end to any play-acting for the time being. And I had no mind to be mixed up with your doings and activities. As I told you by word of mouth, I know nothing whatever about the circumstances surrounding his death; I can give no information about them, and I am not going to be dragged into a witness box merely to say, on oath, that I know nothing. As it is literally and strictly true that I know nothing I have removed myself from interference — you may try to find me, if you like, but you won't.

I should like to say a straight word to you. If, instead of thinking as a policeman, you had thought as a man, you would see that you were committing an egregious blunder in suspecting me — as you did — of being Jack Riversley's murderer. I am not the sort of man to murder another man merely because of a little unpleasantness with him. If I had murdered Jack Riversley every time he and I have quarrelled he would have died more deaths than I can think of. Besides, I have a liking for life, and murderers, as a rule, get caught and get hanged. I do not want to be hanged.

Now I will tell you something else. I said to you and your companion that you must go back if you want the solution of this mystery. I say so again — Go Back! Jack Riversley is dead — and I quoted to you the old Latin tag: I needn't repeat it. I am not going to say a word against him, but I will say this: what came upon Jack Riversley in his dressing room on Monday night was — Nemesis! No man could have lived the life he'd lived without paying his score in the end — he's paid it. If, eventually, you catch the man who ran that rapier through Jack Riversley's heart the other night, you will no doubt be able to hang him. If he were tried on the other side of the Channel, in France, a jury would acquit him. Do you understand me?

Mr. Chief Constable, I am your obedient servant,
MICHAEL MACDERMOTT.

Stell handed the letter back to Marston and said nothing.

"Well?" asked Marston.

"Nothing to say," replied Stell. "Except — I guess he's right!"

"Right? What do you mean?" exclaimed Marston.

"I think this has been what he suggests — a crime of revenge," answered Stell. "I've thought so ever since I heard what Mr. Atley had to say. Probably, this man Macdermott knows something. I wish he'd told us. But now, he won't!"

Marston turned to Wardle with a look which showed his astonishment.

"Hanged if I can quite see what Stell's line is!" he said. "I think — "

"I know what his line is," interrupted Wardle, nodding at the detective. "And I won't say that he isn't right. Stell thinks that Sir John had an enemy who tracked him here — "

"Or — who was here!" said Stell softly.

"Or who was here, as you say," continued Wardle, "and who, as they say, seized an opportunity and did him in! That it, Stell?"

"That is it," replied Stell. "Just that!"

"Well and I daresay you're right," said Wardle. "The question is — who? Now — "

A policeman with a pen behind his ear looked in.

"Young man wishes to see you, sir," he said, looking at Marston. "Name of Spedding, sir — Charles Spedding. This murder case, sir."

"Bring him in!" said Marston. He turned to his companions with a hopeful look. "At last we're going to hear something, I daresay! Let's hope it's something definite."

The policeman presently ushered in a young working man, in his working attire, who carried in his hand a copy of the Evening Chronicle. He looked round at the three men awaiting him. Wardle suddenly spoke.

"Oh, I know this chap!" he said. "Employed at Mr. Whitebrook's, aren't you a plumber? You've worked at my house."

"That's right, sir — worked for Mr. Whitebrook five years now," replied Spedding. "Up at your house not so long since, Mr. Wardle."

"Aye — and have you got something to tell the Chief Constable?" asked Wardle. "What is it now, my lad?"

Spedding unfolded the newspaper and pointed to the paragraph inspired by Stell.

"I read this as I was going home, sir," he said, turning to Marston, "so I turned back and came straight here. Because I can tell you something about Sir John Riversley! Something I saw last night."

"What?" asked Marston. "Tell it! — but be exact, my lad."

"All right, sir — you'll get nothing but what's fact out of me: Mr. Wardle there knows me, and Mr. Whitebrook'll answer for me. Well, it's just this, sir — I've a hobby! Collecting autographs of famous people — and a very nice collection I have too. Actors, preachers, politicians, cricketers, lecturers — all sorts of people — as long as they're famous. And when I heard that Sir John Riversley was coming here, I made up my mind to get his: I've already got nearly every famous actor and actress of the present day!"

"Well?" said Marston.

"So, knowing that he was stopping at the Midland Hotel and having an idea of what time he'd set out for the theatre, I put my best clothes on and went round there last night, soon after six o'clock, to hang about the door till Sir John came out. Well, I hadn't been there so long before I noticed that there was another man hanging about there, too: anyway, there was a man on the opposite side of the street who walked up and down, keeping an eye on the hotel. I came to the conclusion he was watching for Sir John's coming out — and I was right!"

"How do you know that?" asked Stell.

"Because of what followed. Sir John came out at a little before half-past six. He was alone. I went up to him and asked him if he'd favour me with his autograph, adding that his was about the only famous name I hadn't got. He was very obliging — he signed his name, bade me good luck, and went on. And the man on the other side of the street followed him. So did I. I was going to the theatre — into the pit."

"Go on!" said Stell.

"I kept behind. This man followed Sir John right up to the top of the side street — you know, the street at the side of the theatre, in which the stage door is. Sir John turned into that —

so did the man. I saw no more after that — I went to get into the queue for the pit."

"What was this man like?" asked Stell. Can you describe him?"

"Well, it was night, you know. But he looked like a gentleman. He — "

The policeman looked in again.

"Woman wants to see you, sir! Mrs. Capstick, Bolton's Fold, Marradale."

Chapter 7

WHO IS HE?

STELL gave a sigh of satisfaction. Things were beginning to move; to materialise. He turned towards the door as the policeman showed Mrs. Capstick in. A poorly but decently dressed little woman, obviously awed by her unfamiliar surroundings. Like Spedding, she carried a copy of the Evening Chronicle.

"Come in, Mrs. Capstick — take a chair," said Marston. "You want to speak to me?"

Mrs. Capstick held up the paper.

"It's about a piece in this newspaper, sir," she said. "About whether anybody saw this actor-gentleman up Marradale way on Sunday afternoon. Which — "

"Wait a minute, Mrs. Capstick," interrupted Marston. "Then we shall be very glad to hear anything you can tell us." He turned to Spedding. "Tell us what this man you're speaking of was like — as near as you can."

"A big man, sir — big, broad-shouldered man. I was never near enough to see his face, but my impression is that he was clean-shaven. He was wearing a dark overcoat that came down to beneath his knees, and he'd one of those fashionable hats, light grey, I should say, with a black band."

Mrs. Capstick made an inarticulate sound: Marston lifted a finger at her.

"Wait a bit, Mrs. Capstick," he said. "Well, Spedding, you say he followed Sir John all the way from the hotel to the theatre. When Sir John turned into the side street, where the stage door is, where did this man go?"

"Ah, that I can't say, definitely, sir! There were a lot of people about, you see. The entrance to the gallery is in that side street, and there was a big queue there. And I was in a hurry — I wanted to get into the queue for the pit, at the front of the theatre. But my impression is that the man followed Sir John as Sir John made his way through the crowd. You see, sir, I didn't stop to watch — I wanted to get a good seat, and the doors were about to open."

"Very well — don't go, Spedding — I may have more to say to you. Now, Mrs. Capstick," he went on, turning to the woman. "What have you got to tell us? You say you live up Marradale way?"

"Bolton's Fold, sir, number one. Right opposite the old place they call Marradale Hall, sir."

"What are you — what do you do?"

"Since my husband died, sir, I've done charring."

"Charwoman, eh? Very well — now, then? About Sunday afternoon — do you know anything?"

Mrs. Capstick held up her newspaper and pointed to a photograph of Sir John Riversley — in mufti.

"I saw this gentleman, sir, on Sunday afternoon — I recognised this picture as soon as ever I set eyes on it!"

"Where did you see him, Mrs. Capstick?"

"Well, sir, as I said previous, my house is right opposite Marradale Hall. On Sunday afternoon, it being uncommon fine, I was a-sitting in a chair in my doorway, looking out like. I see this gentleman — which he was in a grey tweed suit, sir, with a light overcoat over it — and looking round Marradale Hall. There was nothing remarkable in that, sir, 'cause a deal o' strangers comes to look at the old place. I see him looking at it from the front, and I see him go round the side to the back, and he evident went right round it, for he come into my view again at the other corner — you may be aware, sir, that you can walk right round that old house. He stood at that corner some time, sir, a-gazing into the garden and the courtyard: then he turned to go down Cordingley Street, which is a short cut to the town, sir. And then something happened which I considered peculiar, sir."

"And what was that, Mrs. Capstick?"

"Well, sir, you get to Marradale Hall, in the usual way, through Bolton's Fold — where I live, sir, as I've said — if you come to it from Weatherfield Road. This here gentleman had come that way — I saw him come up Bolton's Fold till he passed my door. But he went away, as I say, in another direction, by Cordingley Street. Now as he walked off there was another gentleman come up Bolton's Fold, passed me, and crossed over to Marradale Hall. He caught sight of the first gentleman as he was walking away, and I see him give a sort of start, like, as if he recognised him, though to be sure the first gentleman had only his back to him. Then he suddenly started out, sharp, as if to follow him and catch him up. But he must have changed his mind, for he stopped short again, and I see him shake his head. And the first gentleman went on, sir, down Cordingley Street, and that was the last I see of him. But this, sir," concluded Mrs. Capstick, once more exhibiting Sir John Riversley's photograph, "this, sir, is him!"

"Well — what did the second gentleman do, Mrs. Capstick?"

"Just what the other did, sir — proceeded to look round the old house. Walked all round it — came back — went along Bolton's Fold again, sir, close past my door, into Weatherfield Road."

"Can you describe him?"

"Yes, sir, and I reckon he's the gentleman that this here young man was telling you about when I come in, sir! He was a big, clean-shaven, broad-shouldered man, what you call a fine figure, and I should say about forty years of age. He'd a dark overcoat on, and he'd a grey hat — one o' these here fashionable hats —

and I noticed something about that hat which perhaps this here young man — you'll excuse me for not knowing your name, young feller? — didn't notice, seeing as it was dark when he saw him. But I noticed it — I'm noticing by nature, sir."

"What was it, Mrs. Capstick?"

"Well, sir, it was a grey hat, such as gen'rally has a black band round the crown. But this gentleman's wasn't black. It was coloured — it had three stripes of colour — brown, blue, and yellow."

"A Colonial!" muttered Stell.

Spedding put in a word.

"He hadn't that hat on last night, though!" he said. "I'm certain of that. I noticed the hat he had on then. It was a grey, with a black band."

"Well, the gentleman I'm talking about had a coloured band," affirmed Mrs. Capstick. "I noticed it particular, because it was uncommon."

"Probably the man has more hats than one," said Marston. "However, it seems to me that you're describing the same man. Now, had either of you ever seen him before?"

"I never had, sir," replied Mrs. Capstick. "Perfect stranger to me."

"No!" said Spedding.

"Then he's probably a stranger to the town," remarked Marston. He turned to the detective. "What do you suggest, Stell?"

"He may have gone by this time," said Stell. "We can make enquiries. But —" He turned to Spedding. "Can you get a day off from your work tomorrow — if it's made worth your while?" he asked.

"If you want me, and it's necessary — yes," replied Spedding. "I've only got to explain matters to Mr. Whitebrook. We aren't particularly busy."

"Very well," continued Stell. "And can you get somebody to join you — keep you in company?"

"I can get my own brother," said Spedding. "He's out of work just now."

"All right! Now do what I'm going to tell you. Come out in the town after breakfast tomorrow morning. Take a look at the principal hotels first — see who comes out of them. Have a walk round the main streets. Look in at the museum — the picture galleries — any of the public places. Drop in at any of the saloon bars of the hotels — look round the centre of the town generally. If you spot the man you saw last night, you keep him in view, wherever he goes, and tell your brother to run here and fetch me. Understand all that?"

"I understand!" said Spedding with a knowing smile. "I'll see to it!"

Stell turned to Mrs. Capstick.

"Now Mrs. Capstick," he said, "you heard all that? Can you do the same thing — or something like it? You'll be paid for your services, you know. Do you know any neighbour of yours that would accompany you?"

"There's Mrs. Lightowler, sir — she would," replied Mrs. Capstick. "You mean — to look round and keep our eyes open for this gentleman, same as the young man there's going to do?"

"Just the same, Mrs. Capstick! And — to let me know at once if you spot him."

"Oh, yes, sir, I can do that — I shall know him, whatever sort of a hatband he's wearing! I'd a good look at his face, sir — a handsome gentleman."

"Very well — off you go, both of you, and keep your eyes skinned in the morning," said Stell. "If either of you spot him, let us know, here, at once."

The charwoman and the plumber went away, and Stell turned to his companions.

"If this man is in the town, we shall find him before noon tomorrow," he said. "If he's left, we shall have to trace him."

"I wonder who he is?" observed Wardle. "I've been about the town a good deal these last two days, but I haven't seen any stranger that corresponds with what those two describe."

"He's probably gone," said Stell. "We can only try what I've suggested."

"There's something you could do tonight," remarked Marston. "You could look round the principal hotels."

"I'm going to," replied Stell. "But you're supposing that this man is a stranger? He mayn't be! There's a population here of three hundred thousand. Mrs. Capslick doesn't know every well-dressed gentleman of handsome appearance in the town! Neither does Spedding."

"I don't think any well-dressed Hatherford man would wear a multi-coloured band round his Homburg hat!" said Marston.

"True — I'd forgotten that," admitted Stell. "He wouldn't. That's why I said — a Colonial. South African, very likely. Well, I'm going to look in at all the likely hotels."

He made a round of smoking rooms that evening, but with no result; he examined various hotel registers and learnt nothing from them. There were numerous foreigners in the town — a hundred at least — and a great many Colonials; Hatherford, as a great commercial centre, was visited regularly by commercial men from all parts of the world. It was not until nearly noon next day that he heard anything. Then, as he was busy in his room at the police headquarters, the telephone bell rang, and in another second he was listening to a voice that seemed familiar, though for the moment he did not recognise it.

"That Mr. Stell?"

"Yes!"

"This is Spedding. Mr. Stell — we've found him!"

"Where is he?"

"Talking to two gentlemen on the steps of the Royal Exchange."

"You're certain?"

"Positive!"

"Keep your eye on him," said Stell. "I'm coming!"

He ran out of the City Hall and hurried along Market Street. As he reached a point opposite the Royal Exchange, the steps of which were just then thronged with business men, he ran into Spedding and his brother.

"Still there?" asked Stell.

"He's there, all right! Come this way, Mr. Stell. There! Do you see him? The tall, big man talking to those two, by the second pillar? That's the man I told you of!"

Stell looked across the street and saw a tall, handsome man of apparently thirty-five to forty years of age, dressed in a fashionably-cut grey suit, who was talking with much animation to two men of about his own age, both well known to Stell as well-to-do Hatherford wool merchants. He took a good long look at the three, and turned to Spedding.

"Now, Spedding," he said. "Be careful! You're absolutely certain that that's the man you saw following Sir John Riversley on Monday evening? Don't make any mistake!"

"No mistake, Mr. Stell! That's the man, as sure as I see you. There's not the slightest question of it. I — hullo, Mr. Stell, there's that Mrs. Capstick coming along!"

Stell looked round and saw Mrs. Capstick and another woman, each attired in her best, coming slowly along the street: Mrs. Capstick was scrutinising every man she encountered. He went forward, and touching her shoulder led her behind the group on the pavement near where Spedding and his brother stood.

"Look across at those men on the steps of the Exchange, Mrs. Capstick," he said. "Do you see anything of the gentleman you're seeking?"

Mrs. Capstick looked; her withered face suddenly lighted up.

"That's him, sir!" she gasped suddenly. "Him in the grey suit — by the pillar — talking to them other two. Oh, yes, I know him. That's him!"

Stell presently got rid of his assistants, male and female, and proceeded to do his watching himself: he felt somehow, that his man, being in the company of two well-known townsmen, was safe. He stood, watching, until the three men came down the steps of the Exchange, and walking up Market Street, turned the corner and went into the Great Northern Hotel. He followed them inside; saw them settle down in the smoking room and left them. They would be safe there for half an hour at any rate, and he wanted to see Marston.

Marston was in his room, at his desk, looking very grave. And in the chair at the side of the desk sat Carroll, looking still graver.

Chapter 8

DIRTY LINEN

MARSTON motioned Stell to close the door; there was something in his gesture which showed the detective that some new thing had arisen.

"Sit down, Stell," said Marston. "Mr. Carroll's just come in to tell me of a discovery he's made. He's given me no details, so perhaps he'll give them to both of us now that you're here." He turned to Carroll. "Let's hear everything," he continued. "Don't omit anything at all — you don't know how these small and apparently insignificant things matter, sometimes."

"I shall have to go back, then," said Carroll, with obvious unwillingness. "It's a story I don't like to tell, especially as a dead man's affected. But I suppose it's got to be told. I don't know if you're aware that we — I mean Sir John Riversley and his company — have only recently returned from a tour in Australia?"

"Yes, I've heard that," replied Marston. "Read it in the papers. Great success, wasn't it?"

"Great! He was immensely popular there. Especially in Melbourne, where we played for some time. It was at Melbourne that the thing began that I feel bound to tell you about. Sir John, of course, was made a great deal of, in society, I mean — no end of social engagements and so on. And — to cut things short —

there was a young married woman whom he met there who — who — oh, well, we may as well stick to the naked truth! — who got, I should say, absolutely crazy about him! Used to come to the theatre every night — got herself asked to every place he went to — always seeking his society — and that sort of thing — you know!"

"And — he?" asked Marston.

"Can't say. He'd a good deal of spare time on his hands. Often I never knew where he was. And — it's useless to deny it — he was fond of women. This was a particularly pretty woman. But, from what I saw of her, excitable, highly strung, neurotic — just the sort of woman to be carried away if she took a fancy into her head."

"Her husband? — you said she was a married woman."

"Yes. Her husband was a Mr. Arthur Wollaton, a man who had something to do with wool. Older than his wife — fifteen years older, I should say. Businessman. They'd no children. He was a very wealthy man — devoted to business. And she'd nothing to do."

"Any scandal?" asked Marston.

"It was developing. Things were being said. I was glad when we left. I believe — though I'm not certain — that Sir John had a letter from Wollaton's solicitors, sort of warning him off."

"Well? — you came home?"

"Yes, but — this is really the thing or, rather, one of the things, I came to tell you about. It's just eight weeks since we got back. Well, a fortnight ago, I saw Mrs. Wollaton and Sir John together in London!"

Stell pricked up his ears. He had been listening with folded hands, but now he got out his notebook.

"Where did you see them?" he asked.

"In a certain restaurant in Soho," replied Carroll. "Brandini's. I happened to be in that neighbourhood and turned into this place for lunch. It's not a big place, and as soon as I'd entered I saw these two."

"Did they see you?"

"No! I went out again, instantly. They were too much engaged in talking to notice anything."

"You're quite sure it was Mrs. Wollaton?"

"Absolutely certain! She's the sort of woman you'd never forget if you'd once seen her."

"Have you seen or heard anything of her since?"

"No! — nothing."

"Did Sir John ever mention to you that she was in England?"

"Not a word! He wouldn't — he would be as close as is possible about things of that sort. But I know that he had something worrying him during the last few weeks. That was easy to tell."

"Bad temper?"

"That — and other things. I've known him — intimately — for years, you see."

There was a pause. Stell made some notes. Then Marston turned to Carroll.

"Well?" he said. "That's not the most important thing? The rest?"

Carroll glanced at Stell.

"No!" he said. "What Mr. Marston means is this — I'd just told him when you came in. The fact is, Wollaton, the husband, is here!"

Stell affected surprise.

"Here? Where?" he asked.

"In this town — Hatherford! I saw him myself, this morning."

"To speak to?"

"No — I never have spoken to him. I only knew him by sight in Melbourne. But I often saw him there, and I knew him at once as soon as I saw him this morning."

"Where did you see him?"

"Coming out of the Hatherford Chamber of Commerce. He'd a couple of men with him whom I know to be prominent businessmen here — Mr. Murgatroyd, and Mr. Jubb."

"You're sure of his identity?"

"Just as sure as I am of his wife's! Positive!"

Stell put his notebook away and turned to Marston.

"That's the man that Mrs. Capstick told us of and that Spedding told us of," he said. "They've both identified him, in my presence, in Market Street, just now. He was on the steps of the Royal Exchange. He'd the two men with him that Mr. Carroll mentions — Jubb and Murgatroyd. Of course I know them — they're both magistrates. I followed the three of them to the Great Northern Hotel, and they're there in the smoking room, just now."

Marston gave the detective a long, enquiring stare.

"Well?" he said. "Well, Stell — "

"We shall have to see him," replied Stell. "We'd better go there, together, at once."

Marston got up. He glanced at Carroll.

"You'll keep all this to yourself, Mr. Carroll?" he said. "It's a miserable business, and there'll be some dirty linen washed in public before it's over, I'm afraid! Well, come on, Stell! If we've got to go — "

"We have got to go!" said Stell dourly. "What else?"

He marched the Chief Constable off to the Great Northern Hotel, and into the smoking room the three men he had left there were still in the corner in which he had left them, smoking and chatting.

"You tackle it!" whispered Stell. "Murgatroyd and Jubb know you well enough."

Marston nodded, and with the detective at his elbow made across the big room. The two Hatherford men looked up and saw him.

"Hello, Chief Constable!" said one. "What brings — "

"Good morning, Mr. Jubb," replied Marston. "Good morning, Mr. Murgatroyd. Sorry to break in on you, but — I believe this gentleman is Mr. Arthur Wollaton, from Melbourne, Australia?"

The three men stared at Marston with varying degrees of surprise. But Wollaton responded promptly.

"That's me, sir!" he said. "But who — "

"This is our Chief Constable, Mr. Marston," said Jubb. "What is it, Marston — " Marston looked round. There were other men in the room, though not near them. Still. . .

"I think we'd better go into another room, gentlemen," he said. "There's a small room in there — reading room. See if it's empty, Stell."

Stell went across and opened a door. He motioned to the others.

"Nobody here," he said as they came up.

"Shut the door, Stell," commanded Marston when they were all inside. He turned to Wollaton.

"Mr. Wollaton!" he said. "I'm sorry to have to ask you some questions. Mr. Jubb and Mr. Murgatroyd are both on our bench, and they're evidently friends of yours, so you won't mind if I speak in their presence? You're aware, Mr. Wollaton, that Sir John Riversley, the actor, was murdered in his dressing room at the Theatre Royal in this town on Monday night? Well, I'm informed that you knew Sir John in Melbourne, within the last few months. Is that so?"

Wollaton responded promptly.

"It is! Quite right."

"I'm informed, too, that you saw him, near the old house called Marradale Hall, in this town, on Sunday afternoon. Is that true?"

"Quite true! I saw him."

"I'm further informed that on Monday evening, after watching for his coming out, you followed him from his hotel, the Midland, up to the theatre. Is that correct?"

"That's absolutely correct! I did."

"Do you mind telling me why?"

"Not a bit! Just to make sure he was there."

"Had you followed him to Hatherford, Mr. Wollaton?"

Wollaton glanced at his two friends, who were listening anxiously. Jubb nodded.

"You can tell Marston anything, Wollaton," he said. "Tell him everything!"

"Well," said Wollaton, "yes! The fact is this, Mr. Chief Constable. When he was in Melbourne, where I live, Sir John Riversley, whom I consider to have been a man of bad character, became on much too intimate terms with my wife. Possibly she was as much — maybe more — to blame than he was. I did my best to stop matters. He left. He had scarcely left when she left, too. I have not been able to trace her, so far, but I believe she came to this country to join him. And I have big business interests in this country, especially here in Hatherford, as the chief seat of the wool trade; accordingly, I came over here myself, to find my wife and to do some business. When I landed in England last Friday I found that Sir John Riversley was playing here in Hatherford this week, so I decided to come down. I arrived here, at this hotel, on Saturday evening. Looking round the old parts of the town on Sunday afternoon I saw Sir John, as you've heard. It's true that I followed him from his hotel to the theatre. I will tell you exactly what was going to be done. Lunching with them on Monday, I took these two friends of mine, Mr. Jubb and Mr. Murgatroyd, into my confidence: they fully understood the position. We arranged a plan for the evening. We took the stage box at the theatre — in Mr. Jubb's name. What we were going to do was this — at the end of the first act we were going to demand an interview with Sir John Riversley. If he didn't give us one, I was going to denounce him from my place in the stage box as soon as he made his next entrance!"

"What did you wish to ask him at the interview?" asked Stell.

Wollaton turned and gave the detective a long look. He glanced from him to Marston.

"Who's this man?" he asked.

"Detective Sergeant Stell," replied Marston. "I was going to ask you the same question, Mr. Wollaton. It's a mutual one."

"I should think you know what I was going to ask him!" said Wollaton. "For news of my wife!"

"You think he could have answered it?"

"Pshaw! Of course he could have answered it! She came here to join him!"

"Well," said Stell, "you followed him to the theatre. What then?"

"He went in at the stage door. And I waited, then, for these gentlemen to join me."

"Sir John Riversley," remarked Stell, "entered the stage door at six-thirty — according to the doorkeeper. What time were these gentlemen to meet you?"

"About seven o'clock."

"What did you do between six-thirty and seven, then?" enquired Stell.

"Hung about — waiting."

"A whole half hour! You had your box booked."

"Just so — but I waited to make sure that Sir John Riversley was safe in the theatre."

"Where did you hang about?"

"Oh — round the corner of the theatre — in front of the theatre — anywhere."

"Did you talk to anyone? Could you produce anyone to whom you talked?"

"I talked to no one. I just, as I say, hung round. Just before seven news spread in the crowd that something had happened. Then came the news of what had happened. I waited till these two friends came, and told them. We got into Mr. Jubb's car and went to his club."

"That's so," said Jubb.

Stell looked at Marston, and Marston grew uncomfortable.

"Are you staying here, Mr. Wollaton?" he asked. "I mean — any longer?"

Jubb interposed.

"As a matter of fact, Chief Constable," he said, "as soon as we three have lunched, Mr. Wollaton, who's been personally known to me for fifteen years, is coming home with me as my guest for a week or ten days. If you want him, you've nothing to do but phone me. He'll not run away, and he'll not be out of my sight."

Marston and Stell went away a few minutes later. Stell was thoughtful.

"I'd like to know more about that quarter of an hour," he said. "How do we know he didn't get in by that private door?"

Marston made no reply: he had been impressed by Wollaton's straightforward replies. They went back in silence to his office. And there they found Pratt, the dresser, awaiting them.

Chapter 9

THE PRIVATE HOTEL

PRATT was still in a lachrymose state: it was obvious enough to Marston and Stell that whatever Sir John Riversley had been to other people, Pratt had regarded him with dog-like affection. He was wiping away a tear when the two police officials found him, and regarding with downcast eyes a parcel in brown paper which lay on his knees.

"Well, Pratt," said Marston, "what have you got there? — something you want to show me?"

Pratt began to untie the strings of the parcel.

"I've been packing the things my poor master left in his rooms at the Midland Hotel, sir," he replied. "This, gentlemen, is the morning coat he was wearing when he went to that little luncheon party to which the Mayor invited him. There's a letter, a note, in the ticket pocket, gentlemen, which Mr. Carroll thinks you ought to see — I showed it to him, and he bade me bring the coat to you, with the note just where I found it. There, sir."

Marston took the coat and drew out the scrap of paper to which Pratt pointed — a half-sheet of notepaper, with a printed address, and a few lines of writing in a bold, loosely formed feminine hand.

"What's this, now?" he muttered. "Look, Stell."

Stell looked over the Chief Constable's shoulder and read:

HATHERDALE PRIVATE HOTEL,
MARKET STREET, HATHERFORD.
Monday.

I have followed you and am staying at this address. You must come and see me this afternoon or I will not be answerable for any consequences. Will you realise that this has come to a crisis? E.

The two men looked at each other.

"That's the woman we've heard about — Mrs. W." whispered Marston. "Sure enough! Here, by George! — but is she here now? Well — we'll soon see to that." He turned to the dresser. "You haven't shown this to anyone beside Mr. Carroll, have you, Pratt?" he asked. "No? That's right — now don't mention it to anyone. And look here! You say you're packing up the things Sir John left at the Midland Hotel?"

"Yes, sir — by Mr. Carroll's orders."

"Well, don't pack up anything further. I want to see everything there — I've meant to go along before now, but I've been waiting to see if any of Sir John's relations came forward."

Pratt shook his head dismally.

"There aren't any, sir! I've heard Sir John say many a time that he hadn't a blood relation in the world. He'd a solicitor, though."

"Do you know who the solicitor is, Pratt?"

"Yes, sir. Mr. Blenkinsop, of Conduit Street, in London."

"Odd that he hasn't come forward," said Marston. "We'd better approach him, Stell. He must have seen the news in the papers, and he ought to have come here at once. Well, Pratt, you do what I say — leave all Sir John's effects alone till I can come and examine them. Perhaps this afternoon. Now, Stell," he continued, when the dresser had packed up the morning coat and gone away with it, "we'll go round to this Hatherdale Hotel. Do you know it?"

"I know where it is," replied Stell, "just round the corner in Market Street. Small temperance hotel. That, of course, is where Sir John Riversley went when he left the Mayor's luncheon party. It's only a door or two round the corner — he slipped in there and was lost to sight — I see now why we got no news of his being noticed in Market Street that afternoon. The hotel itself is over two or three shops — I know it though I've never been in it."

"Well, come on," said Marston. "We'll go there at once."

He locked up the half sheet of letter paper in his desk; together he and Stell crossed the square and turned into Market Street. Between the corner shop and the next Stell paused at an open doorway and pointed to a sign fixed on the doorpost.

"Here you are!" he said. "This is where he turned in. Hatherdale Private Hotel: Mrs. John Rawlinson. That's the proprietress."

He led the way upstairs, pushed open a swing-door and ushered Marston into a square lobby, on one side of which was an office window. A young woman looked out.

"Mrs. Rawlinson in?" asked Stell.

"I can get her in a minute," said the young woman. "What name?"

"Tell her the Chief Constable would like a word with her," replied Stell. "Can we go in anywhere?"

The young woman came round and opened a door at the other side of the lobby.

"If you'll sit down a minute," she said. "Mrs. Rawlinson's close by."

The two men walked into a small room and looked about them — Stell, as was his habit, made a mental note of his surroundings. Twelve feet square. Horsehair-covered furniture. Picture — Landseer — over the fireplace. Another — also

Landseer — facing it on opposite wall. Not over-clean cloth on table. Cruet, of the Victorian age, in centre of table. Two Scripture texts flanking one Landseer; two more supporting the other. Bible on a whatnot in one corner. Religious magazines on small table in another corner. Aspidistra in pot on small table in window. General atmosphere of stewed tea and mutton chops.

The door opened and a stout, middle-aged woman came in, glancing enquiringly from one man to the other. Marston stepped forward.

"Good afternoon, Mrs. Rawlinson," he said. "Sorry to trouble you, but we want to know if you can give us a little information. Have you — " he paused, stepped past Mrs. Rawlinson and carefully closed the door, which she had left a little ajar — "have you a lady, a young lady, staying here? A stranger?"

Mrs. Rawlinson eyed both men over before she replied.

"Chief Constable Marston, I think?" she replied. "And I suppose this gentleman's one of your officers? I hope there's nothing wrong, Mr. Marston. No! I haven't any lady, old or young, staying here at present — I rarely have ladies here; my connection is chiefly with commercial travellers. But I had a lady here from Sunday evening to Monday night. Why — "

"Just tell us all about her, will you, Mrs. Rawlinson?" said Marston. "We've had information that she was here and we want some particulars. Tell us what you know."

Mrs. Rawlinson sat down at the centre table and motioned her two visitors to seat themselves on the horsehair upholstered easy chairs.

"Well," she said, "of course, if it's a police matter — but really there's next to nothing to tell. This lady I'm speaking of — she'd never been here before — came in about half-past eight on Sunday night. A porter from the Midland Station brought her here; he carried her suitcase. I was in the office outside there. She asked if she could have a quiet room for a few nights. I showed her one and she took it. She wanted to pay me there and then, and drew out a purse, and I noticed she'd a lot of money in it — notes. Of course, I didn't let her. She had a light supper and went to bed. Next morning she didn't go out — she was in this room most of the time, reading the newspaper. I had to go out of town that afternoon, Monday, so I didn't see anything myself, but my young lady in the office, Miss Megson, told me afterwards that just before one o'clock this lady came to her and asked if it was possible to get a messenger to take a note — a district messenger, she asked for. Miss Megson got her a Boys' Brigade messenger; this lady gave him a note to deliver, but as she handed it to him herself, Miss Megson didn't see the name and address on it."

"Miss Megson could no doubt identify the particular boy?" suggested Stell.

"Oh, yes — the Boys' Brigade office is close by," said Mrs. Rawlinson. "Well, in the afternoon, soon after three o'clock, a gentleman called in and asked for the lady. Miss Megson — "

"A moment!" interrupted Stell. "You haven't told us what name the lady called herself by?"

"Miss Wilson — Miss E. Wilson, London. That's what she wrote down in the register," replied Mrs. Rawlinson. "'But — I noticed something!"

"What?" asked Stell.

"Well, miss or missis, she wore a wedding ring. However, that was no concern of mine. She was a superior, well-behaved lady, and in my opinion, was in some trouble. She'd a strange, almost vacant look — and she started if you spoke to her suddenly. Nerves!"

"Well?" said Stell. "A gentleman called — ?"

"Yes. Miss Megson said he was a fine, handsome man, a regular swell in his get-up: she thought she knew his face; she fancied she'd seen it somewhere — "

"She didn't know him, then?"

"No! He asked for Miss Wilson. She showed him in here — Miss Wilson came to him. He was with her — alone in this room — for some time. Miss Megson says that she heard sounds which made her think that there was a quarrel or disagreement or something unpleasant. Just before five o'clock the gentleman went away. Miss Wilson had tea a little later. About six o'clock she went out."

"Did she say where she was going?"

"No. I came home soon after that, and Miss Megson told me all I've just told you. About seven o'clock Miss Wilson came in. I was in the office; she looked at me as she passed. I nodded and smiled at her — it's my way with customers. She stared at me as if she didn't know me, or even see me — then suddenly she gave me a queer sort of smile and passed on, upstairs to her room. I noticed that her eyes looked very odd, and that she was as pale as death! In fact, I said to myself that there was something wrong, and that I should probably have some trouble with her, and I made up my mind that I'd speak to her. However, before I'd a chance to do so, something else happened. Just after eight o'clock, a few minutes after, I should say, another gentleman called to see her. I was in the office. He said, 'You have a young lady staying here — I wish to see her at once.' I asked his name. He said, 'Never mind that — she'll know.' Well, she just then came out of the room and saw him. They came in here and shut the door. A few minutes later, she came to me and asked for her bill and said she was leaving. She went upstairs, and in five minutes was down again with her suitcase. She paid the bill — I noticed again what a lot of money she had in her purse — and she and the gentleman went away. And that's the last I saw of her."

"A question or two, Mrs. Rawlinson," said Marston. "Are you a theatregoer?"

Mrs. Rawlinson gave him a decided shake of the head.

"No, sir!" she replied with emphasis. "I am not! It's against my religious principles. I've never been in one of those places in my life."

"And Miss Megson?"

"Just the same, sir. Miss Megson is my niece — educated in my principles."

"You're not familiar with actors and actresses?"

"No, sir — and have no wish to be!"

"Well, what sort of man was this that called for Miss Wilson in the evening and with whom she went away?"

"Why, sir, there's one thing I can say definitely about him. He was an Irishman! A very polite, well-mannered, middle-aged gentleman; very expressive face and soft voice, but the brogue was unmistakable."

"Did Miss Wilson seem to know him?"

"I judged that she did. As soon as she saw him, she motioned to him to follow her into this room. He seemed very kind and attentive to her — took her suitcase when they went out, and so on."

"Did you hear anything of where they were going?"

"No, sir — not a word."

"Did he, or she, ask for a railway guide?"

"No, sir — not here."

"And of course you don't know in which direction they went when they left?"

"No, sir — you see, we aren't on the ground floor. I saw nothing of them after they went downstairs."

"Well, Mrs. Rawlinson, if that's Miss Megson in your office, just bring her in for a minute or two. I want to hear what she can tell about the visit of the first gentleman. Then we shan't bother you any more."

Miss Megson could only repeat what her aunt had already told — and she evidently had no idea of the identity of Miss Wilson's afternoon visitor. And Marston did not enlighten either her or Mrs. Rawlinson. He asked the landlady to say nothing of his visit, and took Stell away. Outside, on their way back to the City Hall, he tapped the detective's shoulder.

"Stell!" he said. "That second man, the man she went off with, was, of course, Macdermott! Macdermott bluffed us at

Mrs. Smith's. Now, what does he know? What did he know, then? Where is he? And is she with him? And — is she Mrs. Wollaton?"

Chapter 10

THE AMETHYST

BEFORE Stell could make any reply to these eminently important questions he and Marston were suddenly joined by Murgatroyd, one of the two men with whom Stell had found Wollaton in company. Murgatroyd, like his friend Jubb, was a well-to-do and well-known man; one of the principal men in the staple trade of Hatherford — a magistrate, a reputable man. And when he joined the two police officials, evidently desirous of speaking to them, they drew up to hear him.

"Just a word with you, Chief Constable," said Murgatroyd. He motioned Marston and Stell to step aside with him into one of the courts which opened off Market Street. "Look here!" he went on, tapping Marston's sleeve. "Don't think me interfering, but, seriously, you don't suspect Wollaton of having anything to do with Sir John Riversley's death? Between ourselves, now?"

Marston made no immediate reply. He glanced at Stell. And Stell turned a stony glance on the pavement.

"Well, you know, Mr. Murgatroyd, you can't say that Wollaton hadn't a motive!" said Marston. "From his own showing he'd reason for jealousy, and for something more — revenge! If I hadn't known you and Mr. Jubb, I shouldn't have felt justified in letting Wollaton go free — I'm not sure now that I oughtn't to have detained him."

Murgatroyd shook his head.

"No, no!" he exclaimed. "No — you'd have made an awful mistake, Marston! I've known Arthur Wollaton for twenty years — so has Jubb. He's been our guest here before today, and we've been his guests in Melbourne. We've had business relations all that time, too — there isn't a straighter, more honourable man going, I tell you!"

"Even the very straightest and most honourable men have been known to kill the seducers of their wives, Mr. Murgatroyd," remarked Marston. "You can read that in history as well as in criminal records."

"Yes — yes!" agreed Murgatroyd. "But in this case I tell you there's nothing of the sort. Besides, Wollaton doesn't know that Riversley seduced his wife — not he! I'll tell you what it is — I know all about it! I've known Mrs. Wollaton ever since they were married, a few years ago. Fact is, I was best man at Wollaton's wedding — I happened to be in Australia, on business, at the time, and he insisted on my filling that little post. I thought then that he was making a mistake, from what I saw of the bride, but I didn't say so. Mrs. Wollaton is a good many years younger than her husband and not at all his sort. She's highly excitable, impressionable, and I should say, neurotic — just the sort to be carried away by a handsome fellow like Jack Riversley. And Riversley — there's no use denying it — was a Lothario! You see, I knew him well enough before he left Hatherford — we were youngsters together!"

"Ah!" exclaimed Marston. "So you knew him? You see, Mr. Murgatroyd, I'm not a Hatherford man. Neither is Stell here. So we don't know any past history."

"I knew Jack Riversley in the old days, before he went on the professional stage as well as I know my own face in the glass," said Murgatroyd. "He was a gay dog then and he got into no end of scrapes. Other men hated him, for he seemed to exercise some queer fascination over women. I knew of several cases in which he caused trouble. I'll tell you of one. Do you know Bateson, the reporter — he's dramatic critic on the Hatherford Observer?"

"I know him," said Stell.

"Well, when we were all youngsters together, there was a little coterie of us, all interested in books, pictures, music, the theatre, and so on, that used to meet at a certain café, now done away with, called the Chrysanthemum. We used to foregather there every night. And there was a very pretty waitress there, with whom every man jack of us was more or less in love — Maggie Spray. But Bateson, who was a young reporter then, was seriously in love with her and wanted to marry her. Well, to cut it short, soon after Jack Riversley left the town, this girl left, too. Clean disappeared, and was never heard of again. But it was always believed that she went to join Jack Riversley. Whether it was so or not, I don't know. But Bateson believed she had."

"Why didn't he go after her — or after Riversley?" asked Stell.

"Can't say — may have done for all I know," replied Murgatroyd. "I'm only telling you that to show you what Riversley's character was — and I believe, from all I hear, he hadn't altered. But as regards Mrs. Wollaton, my belief is just this — I think she went for him! One of these infatuations that such women take, you know."

"Do you think she followed him to England?" asked Marston.

"I daresay! I daresay she's in England now. She has money of her own," replied Murgatroyd. "But if she is in England, Wollaton doesn't know where. And he knows nothing about Jack Riversley's murder! — I'll take my oath on that."

"Has he gone to stay with Mr. Jubb?" enquired Marston.

"He has! And if and when you want him, he'll be there," replied Murgatroyd. "But you'll not find the murderer in him, Marston. Look elsewhere!" He was turning away, but suddenly turned back. "Just another thought!" he said, buttonholing the Chief Constable again. "Look here! Have you made any enquiry into Sir John Riversley's financial affairs? No? — well, if I were you, I would! There are always wheels within wheels, you know."

He went off then, but before he had regained the open street, Stell was at his heels.

"Mr. Murgatroyd — just one question! As you were Wollaton's best man at his wedding, can you tell me what Mrs. Wollaton's christian and maiden names were?"

Murgatroyd smiled.

"Why, I can!" he answered. "Evelyn Wilson."

"Thank you," said Stell, and turned back to Marston. "That was Mrs. Wollaton, right enough, at the Hatherdale Hotel," he said. "She described herself as Miss E. Wilson. Mrs. Wollaton's maiden name was Evelyn Wilson! There we are — and I've got my own theory about the murder, now."

"Well?" said Marston. "What is it?"

"I think Mrs. Wollaton killed Riversley! You know what she said in that note? — that things were at a crisis? Well, I think they'd a row when he called on her in the afternoon — probably he let her see that it was no good following him. I think she went to the theatre in the evening and contrived somehow to get into his dressing room. There they had another scene. Most likely she was desperate — half-mad. And — that rapier lay handy! Probably, as soon as she'd run it into him as he sat with his back to her, she made off — and met Macdermott. You remember that Macdermott wouldn't tell us where he was between six-thirty and six-forty-five, but admitted readily that he was close by? I figure it that Macdermott calmed her down, got her away, and later called for her at the Hatherdale, and took her out of the town. That, now that we know all we do know, is how I work things out. And the question now is — where is she?"

"Yes!" agreed Marston. He stood considering matters for a moment or two; then he moved. "Come along to the theatre, Stell," he said. "We can do two things there. Carroll's still there, and I'd like to ask him the question suggested by Murgatroyd — what about Sir John's financial affairs. And we can ask him, too, if he can help us further about finding Macdermott. Because it's very evident that if we want Mrs. Wollaton we've got to find Macdermott first."

They went up to the theatre. Although it was closed for the week, Jenkinson was at his post at the stage door. He looked out of his window at them, with a silent enquiry.

"Mr. Carroll still about?" asked Marston. Then he suddenly caught sight of Carroll standing at the end of the passage, with Gresford. "Oh, there he is!" he continued, going forward. "All right, Jenkinson — he sees me."

Gresford and Carroll were standing just within the open door of the room in which Sir John Riversley had met his death. They were looking within the room, and they were not alone. Simpson, the head carpenter, was there, and there was also a woman, who, armed with a dustpan and an assortment of brushes and cloths, was evidently contemplating an attack on the room as soon as the word of assault was given. It was at this woman that the two police officials stared as they entered. They had reason. She was an undersized, gaunt thing of some sixty or sixty-five, slightly deformed, and like most deformed people evidently of considerable strength. Stell, who had a genius for observing everything, noted the immense strength of her shoulders and the muscular power of her bare arms. But he was also struck by the extraordinary ugliness of the woman's face — nose nearly met chin; eyes were set close together. The thought flashed through him that she was like nothing so much as those grotesque heads that one sees in Christmas pantomimes. And there she stood, quiescent, dustpan in one hand, brushes and cloths in the other, watching Gresford as a dog watches its master, steadily, silently.

Gresford turned on hearing Marston's voice.

"Oh, I was just going to telephone you, Mr. Chief Constable," he said. "I want to have this room thoroughly cleaned out before the end of the week — there'll be another company here on Monday next. Have you done with it? I mean, do you want to make any further examination?"

"No, thank you," replied Marston. "We've done with it. I looked through it pretty closely myself, you know, the day after — "

Gresford turned to the woman.

"Go ahead, Mrs. Ubbard," he said. "I want it all done by Saturday."

The woman shot into sudden activity, tearing up carpets and rugs; the men retreated into the passage without, and thence to Gresford's room. Marston drew Carroll aside.

"I came to ask you a question," he said. "Can you tell me this, as the late Sir John's business manager. Were his financial affairs all right?"

Carroll smiled.

"Yes!" he said, unreservedly. "Absolutely! Sir John had done well — he was a wealthy man. He made a lot of money out of his visits overseas — the United States, Canada, Australia. He'd no financial worries."

"Do you know if his death would benefit any particular person?" asked Marston. "Do you know anything about his will?"

"No — his solicitor will know. I'd a letter from him this morning. He's ill in bed. As soon as he's up again — in a few days — he's coming down here, to the adjourned inquest. He — "

The charwoman suddenly poked her face in at the door.

"Mr. Gresford!" she said in a queer, gruff voice. "Here! Found it under the fringe of a rug."

She thrust something into the manager's hand and hurried away. Gresford, stretching out an open palm, exhibited an amethyst, set in gold, which had evidently formed the distinguishing feature of a pendant. A bit of gold chain was attached to it.

"Good Lord!" muttered Marston. He glanced at Stell, and he saw instantly that the thought that had come to him was identical with one that had come to Stell. "A lady's ornament?" he said, affecting indifference.

"Let's see — Miss Quartermaine, the famous tragedienne, had that room the week before Sir John Riversley came," said Gresford. "I reckon she's dropped this — I'd better send it to her."

"Um! — would you mind if I keep it — till you see if it is Miss Ouartermaine's?" suggested Marston, holding out his hand. "You see, found where it was — eh?"

He left the theatre a few minutes later with the amethyst in his pocket. Once outside he turned and looked enquiringly at his companion.

"Precisely!" said Stell. "If we can prove that that stone belonged to Mrs. Wollaton we shall be able to form a pretty positive conclusion! Her husband would know."

"We won't go to him at present, though," declared Marston. "All this had better be kept quiet till we know more. Look here, Stell! I'm going to call in at the Midland Hotel to have a final inspection of Sir John's effects there. How would it be if you go round the stations and see if you can find anybody who saw those two — Macdermott and Miss Wilson, as we'll call her — leave on Monday night? Of course, they mayn't have left by train at all, but — it's worth trying. Come to my office afterwards."

Stell hesitated before turning away.

"Let's know — or let me know — where we are?" he said. "Do I understand this? We're to keep all we know to ourselves for the time being, and work, underground, eh, till we get something definite? Well — what about the next step? What do you suggest?"

"What I suggest is that we next get hold of Macdermott and find out from him where Miss Wilson, or, as we believe her to be, Mrs. Wollaton, is," replied Marston. "Try the stations, and meet me in an hour."

Stell turned up in the Chief Constable's office in less than an hour. Marston had just got in. He shook his head at sight of the detective.

"Drew blank at the Midland Hotel," he said. "Nothing whatever amongst Sir John's things there. Had any luck, Stell?"

"I traced them," replied Stell. "They booked from the Great Northern for King's Cross on Monday night, by the eight-forty-five. London! — where there are seven million other folk!"

Chapter II

HEADING OF A LETTER

MARSTON considered this new item of information during a moment's silence.

"Aye, well!" he said at last. "Macdermott's got to be found. We could get out a wanted notice for him, or apply to the Scotland Yard people. After all, being what he is, he's something of a public character. He can't be hidden for ever — he'll want an engagement — he's his living to make."

"He's got money of his own," remarked Stell.

"Mayn't be much," said Marston. "Anyhow, we've got to find him, somehow, for there's no doubt that he'll know where Mrs. Wollaton is. But look here, Stell, before we go into that, there's another thing I've been thinking of since you left me. You heard what Murgatroyd said about that man Bateson, the dramatic critic? Well, what about him?"

"What do you mean?" asked Stell.

"I mean that there's the same motive as in Wollaton's case. Revenge! According to Murgatroyd, Riversley got Bateson's girl away from him. Supposing that Bateson's saved it up for Riversley all these years?"

Stell shook his head.

"I know Jim Bateson," he said. "I know him well — in a sense he's a pal of mine. I should never suspect him. Bateson's too fond of his own ease and comfort, and especially of his pleasures, which, if you want the truth, are eating and drinking, to risk his neck, however much he hated a man. I see Bateson pretty nearly every evening," he continued with a smile. "He and I generally turn in for an hour or so at the Huntsman's Horn; it's the only place of that sort I ever go to. You've got the Hyacinth Club to go to — my club's the pub!"

"All the same, you never know," said Marston. "Bateson may have kept up his jealousy against his old rival. He's a Hatherford man, isn't he? — well, then, he's a Yorkshireman, and the old saying about a Yorkshireman keeping a stone for ten years comes up again. And don't you forget this — Bateson's been dramatic critic for the Hatherford Observer for years, and he no doubt knows all the ins and outs of the Theatre Royal as well as he knows his own house. Is he a married man?"

"He's a married man with a wife and three children," replied Stell. "Lord, no! — there's nothing in that idea, Chief! Mrs. Wollaton's the murderess! What about that stone the old charwoman picked up? Hers, I'll bet! She dropped it."

Marston thought a moment.

"Maybe," he said. "There's something in that. We must try to trace it. God, Stell, what an ugly old witch that charwoman was! Fascinated me. Sort of Mother Shipton. What did Gresford call her?"

"Her name's Ubbard," replied Stell. "I know her well enough. She's worked at the T.R. for over forty years — regular institution. Her name being what it is, they call her Mother Hubbard there. Everybody knows her."

"Damned queer old thing, anyhow!" said Marston. "Well," he continued, pulling out his watch, "I'm off to the club — getting on to dinner time, and I promised to meet Alderman Wardle.

We can't do any more tonight, Stell — we'll see about tracing Macdermott in the morning."

Stell went away — homewards, but intending to call in at the Huntsman's Horn on his way. Glancing across the street as he left the police headquarters by a side entrance he saw Murgatroyd, at the door of his warehouse, about to get into his car. Stell hurried across and hailed him.

"Hullo!" said Murgatroyd. "Any fresh news?"

Stell motioned him to draw aside: Murgatroyd's chauffeur was there.

"Nothing particular," he answered. "I just wanted to ask you a question, Mr. Murgatroyd. You know Mr. and Mrs. Wollaton well, don't you?"

"I know him best, of course," replied Murgatroyd. "He's been over here, on business, two or three times. We do a good deal of trade with him, some of us here in Hatherford. And of course I've seen him when I've visited Australia — stayed with him in Melbourne, as a matter of fact."

"Since his marriage?" asked Stell.

"Oh, yes — stayed a week with him and his wife, two years ago. Jubb was with me."

"Well, look here," said Stell. "Can you tell me — and I don't want it to go any futher — if you've ever seen Mrs. Wollaton wear a very fine amethyst, as a pendant. Amethyst on a thin gold chain?"

Murgatroyd started and looked hard at his questioner.

"Good God!" he exclaimed. "What are you after?"

"Never mind," said Stell. "Have you?"

"I have!" replied Murgatroyd. "And for a good reason. I gave it to her! I told you and Marston that I was Wollaton's best man. Well, that was my present to the bride. I bought it at a swell jeweller's shop in Melbourne. But — what do you know about it?"

"Can't — mustn't — tell you, now, Mr. Murgatroyd," replied Stell. "Pledged to secrecy. But you shall know — I'll promise you that. Meanwhile, much obliged to you."

He turned and went swiftly away, leaving the wool merchant to stare after him. Well — that was so much more ascertained! The amethyst picked up by Mother Hubbard in the dressing room in which Sir John Riversley had been murdered was without doubt Mrs. Wollaton's. So — um! There was a lot to think about.

Ten minutes later Stell turned into the bar-parlour of the Huntsman's Horn, an old-fashioned tavern near the Theatre Royal. It was just six o'clock, and the room was empty save for one man. That man was Bateson. Bateson sat in his favourite corner, a cigar in his lips, a glass of whisky on the table before him, the evening paper in his hand. He was a big, fat man, whose heavy face bore signs of his love of eating and drinking, but whose voice was cheery and pleasant enough when he looked up and saw Stell.

"Hello, Hawkshaw — Vidocq - Pinkerton!" he said. "Eased off a bit, what? What you going to have? Drop of the usual?" He turned to the demure young lady behind the bar. "Mr. Stell's usual, my dear, if you please. And — while you're at it — of mine, too. Any news, Stell?"

Stell dropped into the easiest chair he could find and manoeuvred it close to the fire.

"Nothing to speak of," he answered.

"Still on at that murder business, I reckon," said Bateson. "Bah! — you chaps'll never make head or tail of it! Clever, that fellow!"

"What fellow?" asked Stell.

"Him as done it! — to use expressive though ungrammatical language," replied Bateson. "Well managed! Tracks his man — runs him to earth — pops in — gets it over very neatly — pops out — goes clean away — all over in a jiffy and nobody the wiser. Nobody! — of all the folk round about! Why, I was there!"

"Where were you?" enquired Stell.

"Dressing room, upstairs — talking to two of the company. Right over Jack Riversley's room. There, I tell you — at the time."

"You never heard or saw anything?"

"Not I! None of us. Old Micky Macdermott, he came in while I was there — he'd never heard anything, he told me after, though he passed the door of the room on his way up."

"Oh, he did, did he?" remarked Stell. "Um! Got any ideas as to who did it?"

"Me? Not the ghost of one. But I'm not and never have been surprised. Jack Riversley was a damn bad lot! — women. Always that way. Did me a dirty trick once, Stell — a damned dirty trick. Girl in this town — lovely girl! I'd ha' married that girl — s'elp me, I would. He got her away — Lord knows what became of her — I don't! And, between you and me, if I hadn't been a respectable married man now, with kids of my own, I'd ha' had it out with him before now. But — wouldn't do, my boy, wouldn't do! When you've given hostages to fortune, best thing to keep quiet."

"Did you see him to speak to Sunday or Monday?" asked Stell.

"Did I hell! D'you think I'd speak to a dirty skunk like that? Not me, sir — I'm a gentleman, and Jack Riversley was a damned cad. And yet — we were friends once! Boys together. Ah me — I'm getting sentimental, Stell, but I'd only had two whiskies when you came in. Drink up, my lad, and we'll have another. Hello, here's old Clifton Claye! What ho, Polonius!"

Stell turned, to see a familiar figure emerging slowly from the doorway. It was that of a little, very old man, whose spare frame was completely hidden from view by an ancient ulster overcoat of a pattern well known in the 'seventies and 'eighties, but never seen since, and was topped by a shawl securely fastened about its wearer's neck and shoulders. All that could be seen between overcoat, shawl, and wide-brimmed hat was an old, shrewd face, worn and wrinkled, out of which peered two still bright and alert eyes, full of kindly humour. Everybody in Hatherford knew old Clifton Claye, but nobody knew his age: what they did know was that he was an old actor who in his time had played with Macready and with Madame Celeste, and that he could talk about things that had happened so long ago that any listener might have been excused if he had set the old man down as being nearer ninety than eighty.

"Come on, Clifton!" said Stell, pulling up another easy chair. "Here you are — favourite pew. What're you going to drink — usual thing, eh?"

Clifton Claye made his way across the room with an old-fashioned bow to the barmaid, and sank contentedly into his easy chair. But he shook his head at Stell's invitation.

"No, no, laddie!" he said with a chuckle. "I've drunk with you and with Bateson there often enough — often when the old man couldn't reciprocate. But you're going to drink with me tonight, my boys — the old man's in luck. Look at that, now!"

He had been fumbling in the ticket-pocket of his old coat as he talked, and now he extracted, unfolded, and held up to the inspection of his two companions a brand new five-pound Bank of England note.

"What d'ye think of that, laddies?" he chuckled. "Hear it rustle!"

"Croesus!" said Bateson. "Plutocrat!"

"Had a windfall, Clifton?" asked Stell. "Somebody left you a fortune?"

"Ah, my boy, and there's three more in the box at home!" said Clifton. "Three more cracklers like that — the old man'll be in clover for awhile. But we'll change this," he went on, beckoning to the barmaid. "Here, missie! — you know what we all favour. And cigars — the best cigars: big ones."

"He's been robbing a bank!" said Bateson. "I see it in his eye! Lock him up, Stell, before he gets rid of his ill-gotten boodle!"

Old Clifton laughed, and again fumbling in his pocket, produced a letter.

"They wouldn't trust me inside a bank, laddie," he chuckled. "No — that's a bit of a present from my old friend and pupil, Micky Macdermott — one of the best! He hasn't seen me for years, and he had to hurry away the other night — you know what happened, boys. Ah — a real good sort, is Micky — heart of gold, sirs, heart of true gold. Read that, now!"

He handed the letter to Stell, and Stell's heart gave a big thump within his ribs. For there was an address! — Macdermott's address. He memorised it at sight:

585, PORTSDOWN ROAD, W.9.
DEAR OLD CLIFTON, —

I meant to call and see you on Tuesday, but the event of Monday evening made it necessary for me to leave Hatherford at once. I heard, however, that you are still young and fit, so I am looking forward to a meeting in the near future. In the meantime, drink my health — often. In great haste, always affily, and as usual,

MICHAEL MACDERMOTT.

Stell handed over the letter to Bateson. The barmaid had brought the drinks and was offering him a choice of cigars. He took one, cut the end off absent-mindedly; lighted it.

"So Macdermott's an old friend of yours, Clifton, eh?" he said.

"Old pupil, laddie! I taught Mac all he knows."

"Why should he hurry away on Monday night?" asked Stell.

"His business, sir," replied Clifton. "Not mine! Mac, sir, is a tender-hearted fellow — a sentimentalist. He would be upset, Mac would." He gave the detective a sharp look out of his old eyes. "I heard you were on that case," he went on. "Any news?"

"Not much — nothing definite," replied Stell. "Do you know anything, Clifton? You hear all the theatre gossip."

"Nothing, laddie, nothing. I've heard nothing — but gossip. But if I had heard anything that you'd call anything, I shouldn't tell you, you know! No, no! Let you find out things for yourself, laddie!"

Stell laughed and presently went away, leaving the old actor and the dramatic critic over their cups. Outside in the street he paused, and stood thinking for a moment or two. At his lodgings, close by, his hot supper would be ready, and he was ready for it. But suddenly he turned on his heel and went back across the town to the Hyacinth Club, and asked for Marston. Marston came out from the dining room, napkin in hand.

"Sorry to interrupt you," said Stell. "But — I've got Macdermott's address."

Chapter 12

KNIGHT-ERRANT

MARSTON looked surprised.

"Good Lord!" he exclaimed. "How did you get it?"

Stell explained.

"Bit of luck, that!" he concluded. "And now of course I must be off there. There's the evening train — eight-forty-five. I can catch that and be in town by midnight, and then go to this address first thing in the morning. Don't forget! — Macdermott knows things that we don't know."

Marston nodded his assent.

"Had your supper, Stell?" he asked suddenly. "No? Come with me, then. I'll give you some dinner. Look here," he went on, as he led the detective into the club dining room. "I'll go with you. I've nearly finished my dinner — while you're getting yours I'll slip across to the office and get some money. We've half an hour."

Wardle was at the table which Marston had just left: he listened while the Chief Constable hurriedly explained matters. Then he put a hand in a pocket and drew out a notecase.

"No need to go to the office, my lad," he said. "There you are — fifty pounds in there — that'll do you. Better leave an address with me, Marston, where we can communicate, if need be."

"Great Northern Hotel, King's Cross," said Marston, pocketing the notecase. "But we shall be back before tomorrow evening — if we find them."

"What do you propose to do?" asked Wardle. "I mean — if you do find them?"

"Bring them back here! We want information from Macdermott, and her husband's here, so that's the obvious thing to do. But look here, Alderman — if you should see either Jubb or Murgatroyd tomorrow, or tonight, for that matter, not a word of this to them! Keep all quiet till we get back."

"To be sure," agreed Wardle. "Let me know what train you come on tomorrow, and if they're coming with you. Well — I wonder if we're getting any nearer. I say! — there's one very queer thing about all this that I can't understand. How is it that Sir John Riversley's solicitor doesn't turn up? You'd have thought — "

"Carroll's told me about that," interrupted Marston. "He says the solicitor's ill, but he'll be down for the adjourned inquest."

"Ten days to go before that comes on," commented Wardle. "There should be some legal representative here now. What's being done about the Company?"

"Carroll's winding things up and paying the members off," replied Marston. "Company's no good without Sir John! Hamlet, with Hamlet left out, eh? Well, Stell, we must be off — just as we are!"

Just as they were, Marston and Stell turned out of a taxi cab next morning at the lower end of Portsdown Road, and dismissing their driver, inspected the numbers of the nearest houses.

"Numbered from the other end," remarked Stell. "Odd numbers this side; even, the other. Can't be far off."

He preceded Marston by a yard or two, keeping a sharp lookout for the house they wanted, Number 585. And suddenly he caught sight of the three figures — and of another and different figure — Macdermott. Macdermott was standing in the bow window of the lower floor, his hands in his pockets, looking out. Stell saw him before he saw Stell, and Stell thought that he looked miserable and worried. The next instant Macdermott turned and saw Stell, and after one sharp glance vanished. But when Stell knocked at the front door and the door opened there was Macdermott. He glanced from one man to the other.

"Come in!" he said. "This way."

He led them into the room he had just left, and closed the door.

"How did you find me?" he asked.

Marston laid his hat on the table.

"We'll leave that question, Mr. Macdermott," he said. "The material thing is that we have found you. Now I want you, if you please, to be frank with us. You know who we are. I don't want you — except as a witness, a man able to give evidence. But I'll be frank with you, and tell you what we know. We know that on Monday evening, after the murder of Sir John Riversley, you called at the Hatherdale Hotel in Hatherford for a lady who had stayed there under the name of Miss E. Wilson, but whom we know to be Mrs. Evelyn Wilson Wollaton, of Melbourne, in Australia, and that you took her away and a little later left with her for London. Now a plain question. Where is she?"

Macdermott, who had listened quietly, replied just as quietly.

"In this house!"

"Whose house is this?" asked Marston. "Yours?"

"No. My sister's — Mrs. Clayton."

"Why did you bring her here?"

"Because it was the only place — refuge, if you like — I could think of. My sister is a very good and kind woman — as you shall see."

"We shall be glad to see her, Mr. Macdermott. But — you speak of refuge? Why refuge? Why did Mrs. Wollaton — you admit she is Mrs. Wollaton? Well, why did Mrs. Wollaton need a refuge?"

"Because of her condition."

"What was her condition?"

Macdermott hesitated a moment. Then he motioned his two visitors to chairs on the opposite side of the table, and took a seat himself facing them.

"The doctor will be here before long," he said. "He can tell you what's the matter with Mrs. Wollaton in more technical language than I can use. But I can tell you what it comes to — in a few words. Mrs. Wollaton has lost her memory!"

"Completely?" asked Marston.

"Absolutely! She doesn't know who she is nor where she is. She's perfectly quiescent, in a dazed, dumb, apathetic sort of way, but her mind is — a blank! The doctor will tell you."

"But — what caused it?" asked Marston.

Macdermott sat upright, staring fixedly from one man to the other.

"I should say," he replied, speaking very deliberately, "I should say — shock!"

"Shock of — what?" demanded Marston. "Ah! — but I don't know," replied Macdermott. "Still — shock!"

"Does she know you?" asked Marston.

"No! She knows nobody."

"How comes she to be here, with you, then?"

"Because in her state she's just passive. Don't you understand? She — just does as she's told."

Marston looked at Stell: he was wondering if Stell understood this sort of thing. He himself didn't.

"Perhaps — considering what the Chief Constable's said to you, Mr. Macdermott: that we only want your evidence, and not you — you'll tell us all you know about Mrs. Wollaton?" suggested Stell. "It's got to come out, you know. Perhaps we'd better tell you — Mrs. Wollaton's husband is in Hatherford. But," he added quickly, as Macdermott showed signs of surprise, "he doesn't know that we've come here — he knows nothing of her whereabouts; all he suspects is that she came to

England, after Sir John Riversley, for whom she'd conceived a fascination. Now, what do you know, Mr. Macdermott?"

"Yes, tell us!" said Marston. "You must know something."

Macdermott rose from his chair, put his hands in his pockets, and began to pace the room. Finally, he came back to the table and sat down again.

"I suppose I'd better," he said. "It's bound, as you say, to come out. Well, the truth is this: On the Monday evening on which Jack Riversley was killed, I got to the theatre, that is, to the outside of it, about a quarter to seven. I was just about entering by the stage door when I caught sight of Mrs. Wollaton, whom I'd known, of course, when we were in Melbourne some months ago. She was standing on the kerb, between the stage door and a door a few yards away which was really a private entrance for the management — you'll bear in mind that I know the ins and outs of Hatherford Theatre Royal as well as I know this room. I was astonished, amazed to see her — but there was no mistaking her. As I'd been introduced to her in Melbourne — had, in fact, lunched at her house — I went up to her. I noticed as I got close to her that there was a most extraordinary look in her eyes — she was staring straight across the street as if — well, as if she saw something and yet nothing — can't explain her look any other way, anyhow! Intense — and yet vacant — d'ye understand? I spoke to her. 'Mrs. Wollaton!' I said. 'What are you doing here?' She turned and looked at me in a queer, quiet way — the other look went out of her eyes. Now I knew what had happened in Melbourne — it had become talked about, gossiped about, and I guessed what she was doing there. So, as she made no answer, I spoke again. 'You're not going into the theatre, Mrs. Wollaton?' I said. 'For God's sake, don't do that!' Again she made no reply. She looked at me; she turned and looked up and down the street, as if she didn't know where she was. I spoke again. 'Tell me where you're staying?' I said. 'Is it — ' Now at that point came an interruption. There was a lad of the Boys' Brigade standing close by; he'd an envelope in his hand; I fancy he'd been sent to get seats for somebody and was awaiting their coming with the tickets. He'd heard what I said, and he spoke. I know where that lady's staying, sir,' he said. 'She's at the Hatherdale Hotel, in Market Street; I carried a letter for her this morning, from there to the Midland.' So I lost no time; I took her arm and led her to the top of the street, where there were some taxi cabs on a rank. I put her into the first and told the man to drive her straight down to the Hatherdale.

They went off — "

"Hadn't she spoken up to then?" asked Stell.

"Not a word! She was just — passive, quiescent. She did exactly what I made her do. As soon as they'd gone I returned to the theatre and went in — I was late for dressing."

"Which door did you go in by?" enquired Stell.

"The door I mentioned just now — the private door."

"Why?"

"Because — I've told you more than once how well I know that place — it opens on a passage that leads straight to the staircase for the upstairs dressing rooms. And as I say, I was late. It was the nearest way."

"Did you see anybody in that passage — or at the foot of the stairs?"

"No — and if I had I shouldn't have paid any attention to them. I was too much upset and preoccupied by what had just happened. I passed the door of the room which Riversley was using, and I thought for a second of looking in and telling him what had just occurred to me, but on reflection I didn't, and I went straight on and upstairs."

"Who was in the dressing room you entered?"

"I shared it with two other men — Milford and Harwood. They were there, dressing. Bateson, the dramatic critic of the Hatherford Observer, was with them, chatting — he'd the run of the theatre — I've known him for years. We remained there — only a few minutes, though — talking (at least, they talked: I didn't, for I was thoroughly upset) until a message came that

Gresford and Carroll wanted all of us — on the stage. We hurried there — then we heard the news."

"Of the murder?"

"Well, of Riversley's sudden death, anyhow. Of course, there could be no question of playing. I went away to my lodgings. I didn't know what to do — about Mrs. Wollaton, I mean. Then you came. Well, I don't mind saying it — I did a bit of acting. Perhaps I bluffed you. But I was thinking, hard, all the time. As soon as you'd gone, and as I was dead certain you'd come back, I packed my suitcase, and left. I made my way to Market Street by various side streets and alleys, and went into the Hatherdale Hotel. Mrs. Wollaton was there — still in that passive, quiescent state. She did just what I told her to do — and, to cut it short, we caught the next express to town. I brought her straight here and handed her over to my sister. Next thing was to get a doctor — a really clever one. Well, I know what he says!"

"And that's what, Mr. Macdermott?" asked Marston.

"Loss of memory, consequent on some terrible shock," replied Macdermott. "He'll be here soon — you can see him."

Stell leaned across the table.

"Mr. Macdermott!" he said. "You've been very frank with us. I'd like to know — have you any idea as to what the shock was?"

Macdermott shook his head.

"No!" he answered. "I haven't. You see — I saw nothing but what I've told you of."

"She's said nothing?"

"Nothing! She just sits and stares in front of her, in silence. If my sister gets a word out of her it's merely an affirmative. She's never spoken a complete sentence since I first met her outside the theatre."

"No reference to that?"

"No reference to anything! It's as if everything was a blank."

"What's the doctor say about recovery?"

"He says her memory might come back to her just as suddenly as it went."

"And — could she remember things, then?"

"I can't say. But the doctor will be here presently."

"Well, just one question before he comes," said Stell. "Do you know if she'd been in the theatre?"

Macdermott let out a groan of mental misery.

"Before God!" he said. "I don't! But I'm afraid she had!"

Chapter 13

FIND THE REAL ONE!

A DEAD silence followed on Macdermott's last words. It was broken at last by Marston, who shook his head sadly as he spoke.

"It's a very painful thing, Mr. Macdermott!" he said. "But — that's your impression, is it? That — she'd been in to the theatre?"

"To Riversley's dressing room?" added Stell quickly.

"I can't think of anything else that could have produced this effect," replied Macdemott. "The doctor says she's suffering from loss of memory consequent on a terrible shock. What occasioned the shock? You see, I know a good deal. I know what was going on in Melbourne. Several of us — I mean in Jack Riversley's company — knew. Carroll knew. The poor lady — of course, she's a neurotic subject, highly sensitive, excitable, and so on — was absolutely fascinated by Riversley; he exercised, perhaps unconsciously, that sort of fascination on certain women. Well, evidently she ran away from home and followed him to England, but I'd no notion of that till I found her outside the theatre that night. As to what had happened — but there, don't ask me! I don't know, gentlemen!"

"But I daresay you've formed some theory," said Stell. "Now come, Mr. Macdermott, it'll do no harm to say. Do you think — have you thought — that she killed Riversley?"

Macdermott showed signs of his mental discomfort.

"I don't know what to think!" he answered with a groan. "I — I've feared that it might be so. But if she did, I'm sure she was out of her mind when it happened."

"If she did, that would be the shock that caused the loss of memory?" suggested Stell.

"I suppose so. I can't think of anything else. Though, to be sure," continued Macdermott, "there is another theory one could form — it may have occurred to you. Supposing she went in and found Riversley dead?"

"Before one considers that, there's a point here that I'd like you to speak on," said Stell. "Mrs. Wollaton was an absolute stranger to the town. How did she know how to get into the theatre and to Riversley's dressing room? She certainly didn't go in at the front, enquiring for him at the box office. She certainly didn't go in at the stage door, asking for him at the doorkeeper's window. Both those facts are — facts! The only other way she could get in would be by the manager's private door. How came she, a stranger, to know of it — and where it led?"

"I've thought of all that!" replied Macderrnott. "My belief is that she and Riversley had met during the day. If they did — "

"We may as well be candid," interrupted Stell. "They did meet! Riversley called to see her at Mrs. Rawlinson's hotel. He was with her the best part of two hours. Mrs. Rawlinson wasn't in, but her niece, Miss Megson, was, and she thought she heard sounds of quarrelling. Now possibly, or probably, Riversley told Mrs. Wollaton to see him at the theatre that night, and told her of the private door and where his room was in relation to it."

"Wouldn't that argue that they'd patched up their quarrel — if they'd had one," suggested Macdermott.

"Not necessarily. He may have told her to leave him alone. He may have wanted her to go to the theatre to tell her definitely that things had got to stop, that she wasn't to pursue. The thing to find out is — did she enter the theatre and Riversley's dressing room that evening. If she did — " Macdermott suddenly rose and went across to the window.

"Here's the doctor!" he said. "Excuse me — "

"We must see him, Mr. Macdermott," said Marston. "We must hear what he thinks, from his own lips."

"Certainly, certainly!" replied Macdermott. "But let him see her first. Then he'll be able to tell you his latest conclusions."

Marston nodded his assent, and Macdermott left the room. They heard him conducting the doctor upstairs.

"What do you think, Stell?" asked Marston.

"Difficult matter," replied Stell. "We ought to take her back to Hatherford."

"In that state?"

"Her husband's there," said Stell. "And they've friends there. Jubb — Murgatroyd. She'd be well looked after. And — you never know, in these cases, when the memory won't return. It may come back, I believe, as suddenly as it went. And — we ought to have her handy. If she didn't kill Riversley herself, I should say she certainly knows who did!"

"Maybe that's the real truth," said Marston. "That she didn't do it herself but knows who the murderer is. Hm — suppose it was her own husband, after all? I'll tell you what's a queer thing, Stell, in this case. How is it that as Wollaton was hanging about the theatre he didn't see his wife?"

"Oh, I don't know," replied Stell. "There were big crowds about — queues and all that.

And he may have been in first, and she was in that side street. Anyhow, let's get a clear statement from this doctor. I think we can trust Macdermott?"

"Oh, Macdermott's all right!" agreed Marston. "Sentimental chap, I think. He's played the good Samaritan, anyhow, Stell. Yes — let's see the doctor."

They had to wait some time for that. They heard Macdermott bring the doctor downstairs again; they heard them talking for a long time in the hall. Then they came in.

"I've told Dr. Teape everything," he said. "I judged it best."

Dr. Teape sat down at the table, put his hands together, and addressed himself to the Chief Constable.

"Yes," he said, "Mr. Macdermott has made me acquainted with all the facts. A very, very sad case! Mrs. Wollaton is suffering from complete loss of memory, consequent upon some great shock to the nervous system. She may regain her memory just as suddenly. Now, I understand that her husband is at present in Hatherford with friends. I should advise her removal there."

"She's fit to travel, doctor?" asked Marston.

"Oh, quite! With someone in attendance. Mr. Macdermott tells me that he and his sister are willing to go down with her. She is used to their presence. But I would suggest," continued Dr. Teape, "that you should wire to the husband, or to one of their friends, asking that she — and her escort, of course — should be met at the station and that a medical man should be there, too. I should also suggest that arrangements should be made for Mrs. Wollaton's removal to a nursing home as soon as she arrives in Hatherford."

"All that shall he done, sir," said Marston. "I'll see to everything. But — when?"

"Mrs. Wollaton can be removed any time," replied Dr. Teape. "As I said — under proper surveillance and with care."

Eventually they arranged with Macdermott that he and his sister should take Mrs. Wollaton to King's Cross, to travel to Hatherford by the two-o'clock train, and that Marston and Stell should go by the same train but should not interfere with Macdermott's party. That done, the two policemen went away and to the nearest telegraph office, where Marston drafted a telegram.

"It shall go to Jubb, Stell," he said as he finished writing. "See what I've said? I'm leaving it to him as to whether he brings Wollaton to the station or not. I can trust his discretion."

Stell took the telegram form and read:

Have found Mrs. Wollaton in London suffering from complete loss of memory doctor advises taking her down to Hatherford as her husband is there will you and Mrs. Jubb kindly meet train arriving Hatherford G.N. at 5.10 and bring medical man with you and also arrange for her reception at some nursing home in town use your own discretion as regards acquainting Wollaton with this and bringing him to station. Marston.

Stell handed the form back with a nod of assent, and Marston gave it in, paid the fee and walked out into the street.

"Nasty business altogether, Stell!" he said. "A woman! Let's go and get some lunch somewhere and forget all about it — till two o'clock."

Two o'clock came, and Marston and Stell watched Macdermott and his sister, a middle-aged, comfortable-looking woman, escort a veiled figure into a through carriage for Hatherford, close to the compartment in which they themselves travelled. And three hours later they stepped out at Hatherford to meet Jubb and Mrs. Jubb and Dr. Feversham — and Wollaton. And Mrs. Wollaton did not know her husband, nor the Jubbs, nor Murgatroyd, who came up a moment later, and she clung to Macdermott's sister, turning away from them. . . .

Half an hour later, Dr. Feversham, Mrs. Jubb and Macdermott's sister having taken Mrs. Wollaton off in the doctor's car to a nursing home, Marston, Stell, Jubb, Murgatroyd, Macdermott and Wollaton foregathered in the Chief Constable's private office, with the door locked. And Marston summed up the situation in plain words. When he had finished, there was not a man there who did not grasp his meaning nor one that wasn't reduced to miserable silence because of it.

Except one — Wollaton. Wollaton leapt to his feet with flashing eyes, and brought his fist down with a thump on the table at which he was sitting.

"That's all damned rot!" he shouted. "My wife kill Riversley? Rot, I tell you! Utter rot! She may — perhaps did — have found Riversley dead, but kill him — never! Why don't you find out who did kill him? — you police?"

"We're doing our best, Mr. Wollaton," retorted Marston a little indignantly. "Stell and I have worked hard at this case. We don't want to accuse your wife if we can help it. In the course of our investigations we've had to suspect more than one person — "

"Me, for instance," said Macdermott quietly. "I was the first, I think."

"Well, we'd some grounds, and we didn't know you," said Marston. "You'd had a quarrel with Sir John Riversley. And you played with us, too, Macdermott — you told us you knew nothing — "

"Bluff — for Mrs. Wollaton's sake!"

"And you wrote me a letter in which you reiterated your declaration that you knew nothing — "

"More bluff — and again for Mrs. Wollaton's sake!"

"Well, I'm only mentioning it," said Marston. "I only want Mr. Wollaton to see that we've done all we could. I don't mind telling him that on the first evidence we got — when his name came in — we suspected him!"

"Go ahead — suspect me again!" said Wollaton. "I don't mind. Look here — let's come to it. What grounds — actual grounds — have you beyond what Macdermott says, for suspecting my wife? I'll admit the truth of all he says, just for the sake of argument, but what proof have you that she ever went inside the theatre? Come, now!"

Marston hesitated a moment; then, rising from his chair, he unlocked a safe that stood close by, and taking from it a small parcel, began to unroll the wrappings. Approaching Wollaton, he unclosed his hand.

"Do you recognise that, Mr. Wollaton?" he asked.

Wollaton started.

"It — it looks like a pendant that my wife was in the habit of wearing!" he exclaimed. "If it's the same it was — "

"Given to her at your wedding by your best man — who's here," said Marston. "Well, Mr. Wollaton, this was picked up, with this bit of thin gold chain — look where the chain's worn — in the room in which Sir John Riversley was murdered! What do you say to that?"

Wollaton, obviously taken aback, took the amethyst in his hand, and presently handed it over to Murgatroyd. For a moment they spoke to each other in whispers; then Wollaton motioned Murgatroyd to give the stone back to Marston.

"I can't say anything!" he replied. "It's — disconcerting; puzzling. But I stick to what I've told you — I don't believe, never should believe, that my wife would, or could, murder anybody. She may have entered that room and found Riversley dead, and in the highly hysterical state she was in — "

"That's my notion!" interjected Jubb.

"And — mine!" said Murgatroyd.

"So — who's the real culprit?" continued Wollaton. "You don't know; you've no idea. Now let me tell you mine. This — that there's always somebody who knows, and who can tell, if it's made worth his or her while. I don't care a damn what you police say — I'll lay anything there's somebody in this town that knows who killed John Riversley. And — I'm going to fetch him or her into the light of day! Hear that?"

"I hear, Mr. Wollaton," said Marston. "And — how?"

Wollaton got up and signed to Jubb and Murgatroyd to follow his example.

"How?" he answered with a cynical laugh. "Why, by making it worth his or her while! My friends here'll take me to a solicitor — I shall instruct him to get out a poster, placard, or whatever they call 'em, and handbills, offering a reward for information which will lead to — you know what I mean, Mr. Chief Constable. And I'll make the amount one that'll be worth trying for!"

"It's in your own province to do all that, Mr. Wollaton, it you like," said Marston. "But I hope you tell applicants to apply to me, as well as to your solicitor. What amount do you propose to offer?"

"Five thousand pounds!" replied Wollaton. "Cash down — on conviction!"

Chapter 14

THE BOX OFFICE CLERK

THE solicitor to whom Wollaton was presently introduced by Murgatroyd and Jubb was a hard-headed and hard-featured Yorkshireman. On hearing Wollaton mention the amount that he wished to offer by way of reward for information, he laid down the pen with which he was jotting down his new client's instructions, sat bolt upright in his chair, and stared at Wollaton as if uncertain whether the man from Melbourne was a multi-millionaire and a prodigal, or, more likely still, a lunatic.

"Five thousand pounds!" he exclaimed. "My good sir — preposterous! You mean five hundred!"

Wollaton's face approached the ugly. He smote the solicitor's desk with a clenched fist.

"I said — five thousand!" he vociferated. "Five thousand pounds — cash down the minute the real criminal's found guilty. Don't you see? I want to make a clean, definite job of it! Somewhere in this town there's somebody — perhaps more than one — that knows! Well, I want to get hold of 'em — to make it worthwhile to come forward and tell what they know!"

"There are people in this town — as in all others — that would sell their own mothers for five hundred shillings," observed the solicitor cynically. "Five thousand pounds is, as I said just now, a preposterous sum to offer."He glanced at Wollaton's companions.

"What does Mr. Jubb say? And Mr. Murgatroyd?"

"Far too much, Wollaton," said Jubb.

"Far!" agreed Murgatroyd. "Cut it down!"

Again Wollaton banged the table.

"I want to make sure!" he said. "I want information that's absolute!"

"Look here, Mr. Wollaton," said the solicitor. "You listen to me — and to reason. If there's anybody in Hatherford who really knows anything, you can get the context of all he or she knows for a lot less than five thousand pounds. By offering five thousand pounds you'll only defeat your own ends."

"How so?" demanded Wollaton.

"Because you'll have no end of bogus pretences and claims sprung on you. They'll hinder the real work. In the hope of getting five thousand pounds — Lord, you don't know what some people are capable of inventing. Name a reasonable sum! Say five hundred. I'll warrant you that if there is anybody who really knows, the offer of five hundred pounds'll draw him as a magnet draws a needle. Come — let me put down five hundred?"

"Good advice!" muttered Jubb.

"Quite plenty," added Murgatroyd. "Five hundred's a fortune. A fortune, anyway, to the sort of folk you're thinking about."

"How do you know what sort of folk I'm thinking about?" said Wollaton. "For all you know, the secret may be in the hands of a man — or woman — to whom five hundred pounds is no more than it is to me. However, I'm a stranger, and you know better than I do, and if five hundred brings no response, well, we can increase it. Have your own way."

"*Five hundred pounds reward,*" said the solicitor, making a note. "Information to be given to me or to the Chief Constable. You want this widespread — posters, handbills, eh?"

"I want it doing so that every man jack in Hatherford and district will see it," replied Wollaton. "And as soon as possible."

"It shall be all over the neighbourhood by tomorrow at breakfast time," said the solicitor calmly. "Leave it to me. And it shall be in the local newspapers, too. Well! — you're wise in taking our advice, Mr. Wollaton, about the amount. Do you know what would have been said, by no end of people, if you'd persisted in offering five thousand pounds? Eh — do you?"

"Not I!" retorted Wollaton. "What?"

The solicitor looked slyly at Jubb and Murgatroyd and exchanged smiles with them.

"Why," he replied, "they'd have said that you did it yourself!"

"They'd what?" exclaimed Wollaton.

"They'd have said that you did it yourself and that the offer of five thousand was all bluff to draw attention away from yourself! Got that?"

Wollaton looked disgusted and rose.

"Come on!" he said, motioning to his companions. "You've some nice people here in Hatherford!" he added, glancing at the solicitor. "Not deficient in suspicion, eh?"

"Not at all deficient," replied the solicitor. "Very well equipped that way. Good morning!"

The solicitor was as good as his word, and Hatherford woke up next morning to see posters on every hoarding and handbills in every shop window; poster and handbill displayed in big letters the appealing invitation Five Hundred Pounds Reward.

"He said — here — five thousand," remarked Marston, glancing over a copy of the poster which Stell laid before him. "I suppose Jubb and Murgatroyd talked him out of that? Well, Stell, what do you think of it all — now? We've come to a pass whereat the whole thing needs reviewing."

"Yes," agreed Stell. "But I've been reviewing it ever since we found Mrs. Wollaton and heard what Macdermott had to say. And I think she did it! My impression is that when Riversley had that interview with her in the afternoon he arranged for another at the theatre that evening, and told her how to get to his room by way of the manager's private door, and that they had another row there, the termination of which was that in a moment of mad passion she picked up the rapier and ran him through. After which — she collapsed and lost her memory."

"Well, there's no doubt she's been in that room," said Marston, musingly. "I don't see how we're to get over that. That's her amethyst! How came it there if she didn't lose it there? But — I'm still wondering."

"What about?" asked Stell.

"Suppose she went there and found Sir John already dead — just dead! That would account for the shock. It's possible, you know; just as possible — and probable — as your theory. What I'd like to know, if what I suggest's true, is — who did she see there?"

"She mayn't have seen anybody!" said Stell.

"And she may have seen — somebody! I wonder if she's likely to recover her memory — soon?"

"I called at the nursing home this morning," replied Stell. "She's had a good night and they say seems pretty well. I saw the doctor, too. He says she might recover her memory at any time — but, on the other hand, it mayn't be just yet."

"Well, there's one thing certain," remarked Marston. "Mrs. Wollaton knows something! But does anybody else?"

Stell pointed at the poster, which Marston had already pinned up on his wall. "If anybody does know anything, that'll fetch 'em!" he said. "Hatherford folk! Five hundred pounds? Oh, that'll fetch something out — if it's already there to come out!"

But nothing came during that morning nor during the ensuing afternoon. Then, towards evening, and just when Marston was thinking of setting out for the Hyacinth Club and Stell for the Hunter's Horn, a policeman looked in on his chief.

"Young fellow wants to see you, sir," he said. "Won't give any name or state his business."

"Bring him in," ordered Marston. He turned to Stell. "This'll be some chap after the reward," he said. "Watch him carefully."

The visitor, ushered in by the policeman, found two silent men confronting him with steady watchfulness that would have made most men highly uncomfortable. But he showed no sign of nervousness, lack of confidence, or shyness; on the contrary, he smiled, first at Marston, then at Stell, as if they were bosom friends of his.

"Good evening, Mr. Marston," he said cheerily. "Good evening, Mr. Stell. Fine weather for the time of year, gentlemen!"

"What do you want?" asked Marston abruptly. He had somehow taken an instinctive dislike to his caller — a young man of some two- or three-and-twenty whose generally sly and foxy look was further accentuated by his red hair and light-coloured eyelashes. "Who are you?"

The visitor smiled again.

"Thought you'd know me, Mr. Marston," he replied. "You've seen me often enough, and so has Mr. Stell."

"Where?" asked Marston. "Witness box — or dock?"

"Good joke, Mr. Marston! Neither, sir. I'm in the box office at the T.R. — Theatre Royal, you know. I've had the pleasure of booking seats for both of you, many a time."

"Oh!" said Marston. "Well, what do you want? But — what's your name?"

"Clegg, Mr. Marston — Herbert Clegg. Been at the T.R. three years."

"Well, what do you want, Clegg? To tell something?"

Clegg dived into an inner pocket and fished out a crumpled copy of Wollaton's handbill.

"To ask something!" he replied. "Is this — all O.K.?"

"What do you mean?" questioned Marston.

"I mean — if one did give information that led to a conviction, would one get this money — five hundred pounds?"

"Do you think my name or the name of the solicitor would be on it if it were not all right?" demanded Marston. "Of course it's O.K.!"

"Well — there's nothing like making sure, Mr. Marston," retorted Clegg. "Your name and the other name might have been shoved on just as a matter of form, you know. However, as you say it's all right, I suppose it is."

"Is that all you came for?" asked Marston. His instinctive dislike of his caller was increasing with every minute. "If it is —"

"Not quite all," replied Clegg. "Of course, it's the most important thing to me. I shouldn't like to give away anything for nothing — "

"Look here, young man," said Marston. "Have you got anything to tell? If so, out with it, and no beating about! Do you know anything about the murder of Sir John Riversley? You must! — if you think you've some prospect of applying for this reward."

He fixed a stern look on his visitor and kept it there — but Clegg smiled quietly and shook his head.

"I'm not going to be coerced, Mr. Marston," he answered, with a certain show of independence. "I'm not on oath in a witness box: I can go out of here, holding my tongue if I like. You treat me for what I am, and I'll speak: treat me the other way and keep silence. I daresay I could rake in five hundred pounds over this matter in — another way!"

Marston turned and looked questioningly at Stell. Stell shook his head. He spoke.

"That looks as if you were contemplating blackmail, Mr. Clegg," he remarked quietly. "Think twice! — count twenty, as your Yorkshire saying is. And let me tell you something! If you really know who committed this murder and don't tell what you know, you're putting yourself in a very dangerous position."

"Accessory — after the fact," muttered Marston.

Clegg became serious.

"Oh, well!" he said. "I'll say what I came here to say. I do not know — positively — who killed Sir John Riversley, but I've a very strong suspicion as to who did. And — I believe that with a bit of investigation, I can get the full proof."

"Better hand that over to me," said Stell.

"No! My job! Look here — I haven't a doubt in my own mind, from something I know. All I want is just to find out one little, tiny thing more — a very small thing indeed, but it'll put the finishing touch. When I've got my case complete, then I'll come to you again. But — "

He paused, smiling, and paused so long that Marston, after watching him in impatient silence for a while, spoke.

"But — what? Why don't you say?"

"But if I do come to you with full information, five hundred isn't enough! I shall want double that, at least. It doesn't say on the posters and handbills who's putting up the money, but of course it's some rich man who's interested. Well, if he can afford five hundred, he can afford a thousand. What I've got to say is if I put full proof before you, this man'll have to make special terms with me. I'm not going to sell my knowledge for a paltry five hundred pounds, Mr. Marston!"

"If you know anything — " began Marston.

"You can't prove that I know anything and you can't look into my brain to see what I do know!" retorted Clegg impudently. "I hold the cards, gentlemen — so goodnight till I see you again."

He was gone the next instant, and Marston once more looked at Stell.

"Shall we see him again?" he said. "Or is it all brag?"

"We shall see him again," replied Stell. "He knows something. Give him rope."

They both saw Clegg again that night — Marston first. He was playing billiards at the Hyacinth Club at ten o'clock when a message came to him that a young man had collapsed and died in a street near the Theatre Royal. Marston hurried off there at once and found that the dead man had been carried into a chemist's shop close to where he had fallen. On seeing the body he recognised it as that of Herbert Clegg.

Chapter 15

AT WHOSE HAND?

THERE were half a dozen men in the chemist's shop when Marston got there — the chemist himself, Dr. Feversham, whose house and surgery were close by, a couple of policemen, a couple of young men who looked like clerks or shop assistants. Clegg lay on a sofa in an inner room. He was dead enough — it needed but one glance to see that. And when Marston had taken that glance, Feversham drew him aside.

"This man has been poisoned!" he said in a low voice. "I'm certain of it! So is Wilson — this chemist. What particular poison I don't know — we shall find that out at the postmortem. But that's a fact, Marston! Poisoned!"

Marston looked round at the assembled men. He was in a mental whirl — it was not many hours since he and Stell had seen Clegg very much alive. Now . . .

"Who found him?" he asked. "Who knows anything?"

One of the policemen pointed to the two young men.

"They picked him up, sir," he said. "Then they fetched me from the corner."

The elder of the two young men stepped forward.

"We saw him fall, Mr. Marston," he said. "We were turning down this street, where we both lodge, when we saw Clegg —"

"You knew who he was?" interrupted Marston.

"Yes, sir — we knew him well enough; he lodged close by us. We saw him cross the street from the other side — from the corner, in fact. He was some yards in front of us and he didn't see us, as far as we know. Just as he got opposite this place, Mr. Wilson's, he sort of stumbled — we thought he'd tripped at the kerb. He threw up his arms — a stick dropped out of one hand — and it seemed to me that he clutched at his throat. Then he tumbled all of a heap on the pavement. We ran up; he was writhing. But — it was all over in a second after that. He gave a deep groan and collapsed — relaxed, you know, and lay perfectly still. Never moved again!"

"Well?" asked Marston.

"Well, sir, one of us ran to the top of the street, to seek a policeman; the other rang Mr. Wilson's bell — the shop, of course, was closed. The policeman came — that one — and Mr. Wilson opened his door and we carried Clegg in. That's all we know, Mr. Marston."

"He was quite dead when he was brought in here," remarked the chemist.

"He was dead when I got to him," said the policeman.

Marston turned to the young man who had spoken first.

"You say you both knew him?" he asked. "What do you know about him?"

"We knew he was employed as a clerk in the box office at the Theatre Royal, and that he lodged at Mrs. Sharp's, down this street — number twenty-one. We can't say that he was exactly a friend of ours — an acquaintance. We used to talk to him sometimes, and he was a member of a little club that we belong to. This is a lodging-house street, Mr. Marston — there are a lot of young fellows of our sort in this street — clerks, shop assistants, salesmen."

"I see — well, do either of you know the Hunter's Horn Tavern?" asked Marston. "Well, one of you run there quick, and see if Detective Sergeant Stell is there, in the parlour. If he is, bring him here. If he isn't, run to his rooms — 37, Wellington Place — and tell him I want him."

One of the two shot off; Marston, after a word to the doctor and the policemen, motioned the other to follow him outside.

"Take me to where Clegg lodged," he said. "What's the landlady's name? — Mrs. Sharp. Very good — Mrs. Sharp."

Mrs. Sharp, an elderly, careworn-looking woman, answered Marston's knock at the door. Bidding his guide wait, he went into the dimly-lighted passage.

"I don't want to alarm you, Mrs. Sharp," he said, "but I'm the Chief Constable — Mr. Marston. There's been an accident to your lodger, Clegg —"

Mrs. Sharp started.

"Serious, sir?" she asked.

"Very serious, Mrs. Sharp." Then, seeing that she was not likely to suffer from sudden news, he went on. "The fact is, it's — fatal. He's dead!"

"Dear, dear, dear, sir!" exclaimed Mrs. Sharp. "You don't say! Why, he was full of life and spirits when he was in here for his tea, and he went out whistling!"

"What time was he in, Mrs. Sharp?"

"About six, sir. He went out again at seven — as he always did. Never spent his evenings indoors — I mean when he had an evening off from his work at the theatre, which he had one night a week. Usually, of course, he had tea at five and went to the theatre at half past. Today was his night off. What was the matter, sir?"

"Can't say just now, Mrs. Sharp: you'll hear in time. I called in to let you know, and to say that, of course, he won't be brought here. But now, a question — did he tell you where he was going when he went out this evening?"

"Oh, no, sir, he never told me anything! He wasn't that sort, sir. A reserved young gentleman — very close, sir."

"You've no idea where he went?"

"Oh, none, sir! — none whatever."

Marston went away and rejoined his guide.

"Now come and show me exactly where Clegg was when you first saw him," he said. "You say he crossed this street — was it from that top right-hand corner from where we are now?"

"That's it, sir — as if he'd come round the corner from Challingham Road."

"Was he walking steadily?"

"He was walking fast, sir, and swinging a stick. I've an idea that he was humming a song. He — he went all of a sudden, just as my friend told you."

Marston walked up to the top of the street. Challingham Road was a main street of the city; the Theatre Royal was in it, some thirty yards away from where he stood: Thornholme Street, where he and Stell had visited Macderrnott, opened on the opposite side to the theatre.

"This is where he was when we first saw him, Mr. Marston," said his guide. "We were across there. He crossed over in a slanting line and fell right opposite Mr. Wilson's door."

Stell suddenly came round the corner, the other young man with him. Marston drew him aside; then turned to the two clerks.

"Go and give your names and addresses to the policeman in there," he said, pointing to the chemist's. "You'll be wanted at the inquest. Much obliged to you. Stell!" he went on, when they were alone, "that fellow Clegg was picked up dead, just there, by those two tonight. His body's in that shop — the chemist's — and the chemist and Feversham say that there's no doubt he was poisoned! Now then . . ."

Stell's usual imperturbability suffered a shock. He stared at Marston and from him to the places indicated as if he could scarcely believe his ears.

"Clegg!" he exclaimed. "Dead? — poisoned? Why — "

He paused as Marston gripped his arm.

"Stell!" said Marston, "that's the work of Sir John Riversley's murderer! Whoever it was that murdered Riversley has murdered Clegg! To silence him, of course. Clegg must have gone to the man he suspected tonight. Well, he's paid for it! But what does it show us? That we're up against a particularly cool, determined hand. Now then — who?"

"Clegg's movements tonight?" said Stell. "That's the first thing."

"I've just been to his lodgings — Mrs. Sharp, number twenty-one, down this street," replied Marston. "Nothing to be learnt there. He went in to his tea at six, and at seven went out again, in good spirits, whistling. Of course she doesn't know where he went. Well — we can guess to whom he went!"

"If he did, and if this man succeeded in poisoning him — " began Stell.

"What else?" exclaimed Marston. "That is it, of course. Probably Clegg, bearing in mind his interview with us, went, after leaving his lodgings, to the man he suspected, with a view of blackmailing him. Do you remember what Clegg said when I bullied him a bit? 'I daresay I could rake in five hundred pounds over this matter in another way!' That's what he said. What was he hinting at? Blackmail, Stell, blackmail! Well — he's tried it, and he's paid for it. But — there's a diabolically clever murderer somewhere about!"

Stell said nothing. He was taken all aback.

"And of course that knocks the Mrs. Wollaton theory — at least as regards her own personal guilt — all to pieces," continued Marston. "The whole thing is of a deeper complexion than we've reckoned for, and we shall have to start afresh. And what's to be done first?"

"Trace Clegg's movements from the time he left his lodgings at seven o'clock this evening," said Stell promptly. "I'll see to that — straight off."

But when midnight came Stell had not traced any movement: Clegg had not been to the young men's club of which he was a member, nor to a certain tavern of which he was a frequenter: Stell could get no news of him. He got some, however, before nine o'clock next morning. A man called on him while he was at breakfast.

"I heard just now that you're making enquiries about that young Clegg, Mr. Stell," he said. "I can tell you something. I saw him last night."

"What time — and where?" asked Stell.

"It would be half-past eight. He was at the door of 23, Thornholme Street — Mrs. Milford's. Mrs. Milford, you know, is wardrobe keeper at the theatre, and she takes in actors as lodgers as well."

"Did Clegg enter?" enquired Stell.

"I saw Mrs. Milford open the door to him — he went in."

"See him leave?"

"I didn't. Saw no more than what I've told you. But I saw that."

"Who are you? — where do you live?" asked Stell.

"My name's Matthew Clough — I live at 20, Thornholme Street, right opposite Mrs. Milford. Me and my wife, we let rooms to the theatrical profession — nearly all of us in Thornholme Street do, you know. Convenient to the theatre."

"And you say Mrs. Milford lets rooms as well as looks after the wardrobe at the theatre?" said Stell.

"Yes, but she only takes in one or two lodgers. Mr. Carroll, who was manager to Sir John Riversley, is lodging with her now."

Stell considered all this in silence for a moment or two.

"All right, Mr. Clough," he said at last. "Much obliged to you. Will you just keep what you've told me strictly to yourself for a while? Thank you — it doesn't do to talk too much, you know. You understand?"

Clough said he understood, well enough, and went away, and Stell, finishing his breakfast, pondered over the information. He knew that Carroll was remaining in Hatherford to wind up Sir John Riversley's affairs, but he had not known where he was living. Now he knew, and presently he went round to Number 23, Thornholme Street.

Mrs. Milford herself opened the door to him: Stell recognised her as the big, once strikingly handsome woman he had often seen in Challingham Road but of whose identity he was ignorant. He put his professional card into her hand; she showed no surprise.

"To see me?" she asked.

"Well, yes, Mrs. Milford," replied Stell, "and — I hear you've got Mr. Carroll staying here? Perhaps — "

She motioned him to enter, and opening a door, revealed Carroll at breakfast; Stell saw, too, that Mrs. Milford was breakfasting with him. Carroll, like Mrs. Milford, showed no surprise at Stell's visit. He offered a seat, and a cup of coffee.

"No, thanks," said Stell. "Just finished my own breakfast. I called," he went on, turning to Mrs. Milford "to ask a simple question. You've heard of what's happened to young Clegg, of the box office at the theatre? Well, I'm trying to clear up his movements of yesterday evening. I've been informed, Mrs. Milford, that he was seen to enter your house last night, about half-past eight. Is that so?"

Mrs. Milford, who had resumed her place at the breakfast table, nodded a ready assent.

"That's so, Mr. Stell," she replied. "He did call here about that time — he wanted to see Mr. Carroll. But Mr. Carroll wasn't in. Clegg — whom I've known, of course, ever since he came to the theatre — he's been there three or four years, and I've been twenty! — came in for a few moments, chatting. Then he went away."

"Didn't stay long, then, Mrs. Milford?" asked Stell.

"Perhaps ten minutes. He'd certainly gone by a quarter to nine."

"Did you see anything of him last night?" enquired Stell, turning to Carroll.

"No! — nothing. I was down at the theatre part of the time," replied Carroll, "I'd some business with Gresford. But I didn't see Clegg at all — I know he'd one night a week off. Is it true that he was really poisoned?"

"The doctors say he died from poisoning," replied Stell. He turned to Mrs. Milford again. "Can you remember what he talked to you about while he was here, Mrs. Milford?" he asked. "Did he, for instance, say anything about the Riversley case?"

Mrs. Milford shook her head in a decided negative.

"He did not!" she answered. "The only thing he spoke of was this new piece that starts on Monday — a piece they're going to try out here."

"You've no idea where Clegg was going when he left you?" asked Stell.

"Not the remotest!" replied Mrs. Milford. "All I know about him and his call is that he happened to mention that it was his night off. Well — it was mine, too — or I shouldn't have been at home. No — beyond that, I know nothing of Clegg."

Chapter 16

POTENTIAL BLACKMAIL

STELL saw that there was nothing to be learnt there, and he rose to go. But at the door of the parlour he turned, to speak to Carroll.

"Staying much longer, Mr. Carroll?" he asked.

"I'm staying to clear things up," answered Carroll. "Just as easy from here as from anywhere else. The company's being disbanded — no use at all, of course, without Sir John. I shall be here a week or two yet. Getting on at all with your enquiries?"

Stell made a face indicative of doubt.

"Can't say," he answered. "We don't get much further. I suppose you've not heard anything?"

"I? Good Lord, no!" exclaimed Carroll. "What should I hear? But I say — this Clegg affair? Do you think that's sprung out of the other?"

"Can't say — it's a difficult question," replied Stell. "Possibly! We're all in the dark about that, yet. You knew Clegg, of course?"

"Scarcely. Seen him in the box office, that's about all."

Mrs. Milford shook her head.

"I knew Clegg — well enough!" she remarked. "He was a little busybody!"

"Interfering?" suggested Stell.

"He was what I say — a busybody," replied Mrs. Milford. "Always shoving his nose into other people's affairs. Sly, too — and he'd a bad tongue. You'll not find anybody that had a good word to say for him."

"Likely to have enemies, then?"

"Plenty, I should say. Nobody at the theatre liked him, anyway. Ask Gresford!"

Gresford was the next person Stell called on. But Gresford knew nothing. He agreed with Mrs. Milford, however.

"Clegg, poor chap, was what these Yorkshire folk call a fusspot," he said. "He was always interfering in something. He created unpleasantness at the theatre by his fussiness more than once. I'd have got rid of him some time ago but for the fact that he was a thoroughly good clerk — best we ever had. I don't think he could help his interfering habits — it was born in him. The worst of it was that he used to butt in on matters that weren't in his province! No, I haven't the ghost of a notion as to why anybody should want to get rid of him. Dislike him, yes — plenty of people did. But murder! — that's a very different thing."

"Well, there's no doubt he was poisoned," said Stell. "And there seems to be no reason why he should have committed suicide."

"I'm jolly well certain it wasn't that!" exclaimed Gresford. "Clegg was too fond of existence, and he'd ambitions. No — somebody's had his knife into him. But who?"

Stell left that unanswered and went off to see Marston. And Marston had a young man with him, and he beckoned Stell into the room.

"Come in, Stell — I was just going to send for you," he said. "This man has something to tell us about Clegg — he's only just come in. What's your name?" he asked, turning to the caller. "Who are you? Address, too?"

"My name's Holmes, Mr. Marston — Charles Holmes. I live at Mrs. Sharp's, where Herbert Clegg lodged — I lodge there, too. I'm at Chillingside & Warriner's, wool merchants — I'm a clerk there. They'll answer for me, sir. You can depend on anything I say, Mr. Marston."

"Well, what can you say? Anything about Clegg's murder?"

"Nothing about his murder, sir! But I can tell you a few things that may have something to do with it. Clegg and myself, we shared a room at our lodgings — we've done that for over two years. Of course, we saw a good deal of each other — used to talk a lot at night. Now of late — in fact, ever since the murder at the theatre — Clegg's talked a lot in a queer way about the mystery of Sir John Riversley's death. Seemed to suggest, you see, sir, that he could say something about it . . . if he liked. Well, the last day or two, he got a bit more, not exactly confidential, but more — well, precise. And the morning of the day he was found dying in our street — " "Yesterday morning, you mean," said Marston.

"Yes, sir — yesterday morning. Yesterday morning, when we were dressing, he said a certain thing to me that's made me think a lot — since I heard of his death, that is. Something very queer, Mr. Marston."

"Well — what was it?"

"Well, he was talking, as usual, about Sir John Riversley's murder, and in such a way that at last I spoke straight out. 'I'll tell you what it is, Herbert,' I said. 'It strikes me that you either know who did it, or have a very strong suspicion in that way! Out with it now! 'I said. 'It'll go no further, Herbert.' 'Well, Charlie,' he said, 'if you want the truth, I believe I do know who did it, and I could put my hands on him in half an hour!' 'You really think that?' I said. I do think it!' he said. 'Well,' said I, if you really do, Herbert, why don't you go and tell the police?' 'Ah!' he said, chuckling, that's what you'd do, I suppose?' 'I should so!' said I. 'Why, there's five hundred pounds reward offered!' 'Bah!' he said. Five hundred pounds! What's five hundred pounds? I should want more than that, my lad. If my suspicions are right — and I'm damned certain they are — I could get a darned sight more than five hundred pounds to keep my mouth shut!" You mean — from the man you suspect?' I said. 'Never mind who from, Charlie,' he said. 'I could get it — a good deal more. Silence is worth more than speech, sometimes.' 'Well, you know what they call that, Herbert?' I said. 'They call it blackmail!' 'Damn what they call it!' he said. 'Nobody'd ever know.' 'And there's another thing,' I said. 'I know a bit about law, because I was once office boy in a solicitor's office. If it was ever found out that you knew who'd killed Sir John Riversley and had done what you suggest — taken money from the murderer as the price of your silence — you'd — well, you'd catch it hot and strong, Herbert.' Wasn't I right, Mr. Marston?"

"Quite right, my lad, quite right! You put it quite properly to him. Well, what did he say?"

"Well, sir, if you want to know, he said 'Oh, damn all that! — that's in the clouds. I'm not going to sell my knowledge for a miserable five hundred pounds. If the police would spring it to two thousand, now, I might do business, but not for live hundred! And, of course,' he went on, 'it isn't the police that's offering the five hundred — it's somebody behind 'em. Anyhow, I shall see, Charlie,' he said. 'But I'm so certain of my knowledge that I'm going to squeeze every possible penny out of it! Knowledge is an asset, my boy!'"

"That all he said, Holmes?" asked Marston.

"That's all, sir. He went down to his breakfast then, and when I got down to mine he'd finished his and gone out so I never saw him again."

"He didn't give you any idea as to the identity of the person he suspected?"

"Not the least, sir. All I gathered was that he was convinced of the guilt of some particular person."

"You haven't any suspicion, yourself, Holmes, as to who that person may be?"

"No, Mr. Marston, indeed I haven't! Clegg was a great deal too sharp to give anything away! I was surprised that he said as much as he did to me — but then, of course, we were great friends."

"Have you any knowledge of Clegg's movements on the night he was found dying — last night?" asked Stell. "Did he say anything to you about seeing anybody; calling on anybody?"

"No! He said nothing but what I've just told Mr. Marston."

"And that," remarked Marston, turning to Stell, "amounts to just this — that Clegg believed he knew who the murderer of Sir John Riversley was and that he could get more from him for his silence than he could get from us by splitting! Well, that seems to argue that the man he suspected was not without means! All right, Holmes — much obliged to you for coming; we'll make what use we can of your suggestion, or information. Can you think of anything else?"

"Nothing, sir, except this. Clegg had a box in our room which he always kept locked. He'd papers and things in it. How would it be to examine it, sir?"

"Good idea! Stell, you'll see to that. I say!" he continued when Holmes had gone away. "If what that chap has told us is true — and I see no reason to doubt his story — the man Clegg had in view must, as I've just said, be a wealthy man. Well, Wollaton is a wealthy man! Is it possible — "

"I thought of him — instinctively," said Stell. "There is this much to remember — Wollaton was about the theatre on the night of Riversley's murder for some time, waiting for his friends. Was it he that Clegg had in mind?"

"If you could only trace the whole of Clegg's movements last night," said Marston. "There's an interval of — how long? — between his leaving Mrs. Milford's and his collapse in the street?"

Stell pulled out his notebook and consulted a certain page.

"Clegg's movements last night were these, as far as I've been able to trace them," he said. "He went to his lodgings for tea at six o'clock. He went out again at seven. He called at Mrs. Milford's at about half-past eight, and left her a quarter of an hour later. So I want to know — where was he, and with whom, between seven and eight-thirty, and eight-forty-five and ten-fifteen?"

"Well, there's one thing you can find out at once," remarked Marston. "You can find out where Wollaton was last night at those times? Don't forget — Wollaton is in charge of Jubb! Jubb pledged his word. See Jubb!"

Stell knew where Jubb would be likely to be found at that hour of the morning — at the Exchange. He went there at once. And there was Jubb — and there, not far off amongst the groups of business men, was Murgatroyd, and with Murgatroyd was Wollaton.

Stell waited until Jubb had detached himself from the man to whom he was talking when the detective entered and then approached him. But Jubb had seen Stell, and was coming to him, his thumbs in the armholes of his waistcoat. He gave Stell an enquiring look.

"Now, my lad!" he said. "What do you want here?"

"To ask a question, Mr. Jubb," replied Stell. He knew Jubb, and he went straight to the point. "Can you tell me where Mr. Wollaton was last night?"

Jubb took the detective by the elbow, and twisting him round pointed to where Wollaton and Murgatroyd stood near one of the central pillars of the big building talking to a group of merchants.

"D'ye see Wollaton there, my lad?" he asked. "Have you got your eyes on him?"

"I see him!" replied Stell. "I've got my eyes on him!"

"Well, so have I!" said Jubb. "And I've never had 'em off him, except when he was in bed, ever since Marston entrusted him to my keeping. He's never been out of my sight. Last night —

well, as he's staying with me, he dined with me, and he played billiards with me, and he played bridge with me and my wife and a friend of ours, and when we went to bed, he went to bed. That do?"

"That'll do very well, Mr. Jubb, thank you," answered Stell. "It wasn't Wollaton, anyway!"

"What wasn't Wollaton?" demanded Jubb.

"Somebody poisoned that chap Clegg last night," said Stell. "You've heard of it, of course. That's all! — but whoever it was did it because Clegg knew or thought he knew who murdered Sir John Riversley!"

"You think that?" asked Jubb.

"What else? Clegg did know something. And except for one quarter of an hour I can't find out where Clegg was last night. Thank you, Mr. Jubb."

He went off, leaving Jubb to stare after him, and went into Market Street, to go back to Marston. And in Market Street he came face to face with Mrs. Milford, who was evidently on a shopping expedition.

Mrs. Milford stopped him.

"Heard anything yet, Mr. Stell?" she asked. "No? — well, neither have I, though I've been making an enquiry or two, especially at the theatre. Clegg was never in there last night, after half-past five: it was his evening off, you know. But, Mr. Stell, have you thought of something else? There are some queer things in this case, you know, Mr. Stell! What about that woman that followed Sir John from Australia?"

"What do you know about her?" asked Stell, taken aback.

"Oh, I know! Mr. Carroll has told me a good deal. And my friend Mrs. Rawlinson, who keeps the little hotel across the street there, has told me a good deal more. That woman — why, I know her name! Mrs. Wollaton, she came here the weekend Sir John came, and put up at Mrs. Rawlinson's under a false name, and Sir John called to see her there. And she went out at six o'clock the evening of the murder and came back hurriedly and left — and who with, do you think? Why, with Macdermott, the actor! — from the description I got of him at Mrs. Rawlinson's. Come, now, Mr. Stell!"

"You seem to know a lot!" remarked Stell.

"I know more than that!" said Mrs. Milford, with a significant look. "And I'll tell you something else that I know. That woman's husband is in this town! He's been here ever since Sir John came. Do you know — "

"Mrs. Milford!" interrupted Stell. "I know all you've just told me! Now do me a favour! Keep quiet — don't talk. This is a stiffer job than you think for!"

He turned away without awaiting a reply and went straight back to Marston. And Marston again had company — an elderly, anxious-faced man.

"Stell!" said Marston. "This gentleman is Mr. Withers, the late Sir John Riversley's solicitor."

Chapter 17

WHERE ARE THE SECURITIES?

THE detective inspected the solicitor with some curiosity; the solicitor, with equal interest, inspected the detective.

"One of your — helpers?" asked Mr. Withers.

"Detective Sergeant Stell is in charge of this case," replied Marston. "A very trying and baffling case, Mr. Withers! You've read all about it in the papers, of course? We've been hoping to see you here — why, every day since it happened."

"Yes, yes!" said Mr. Withers. "But you see, I have been very ill — very ill indeed, and away from my office. For some days I was too unwell to read the papers or to have them read to me. I am an old bachelor, you see, Superintendent, living in a London flat with no one but a manservant to attend to me, and — and while I was ill I heard nothing. You will scarcely credit it, but I knew next to nothing about this most deplorable affair until yesterday, when I was able to go to my office for the first time for many days. There is no doubt, eh? — that Sir John Riversley was murdered?"

"None, sir!" said Marston. "None!"

"Dear, dear! And you have — so far — not succeeded in tracing the murderer?"

"We have not arrested anyone, Mr. Withers."

"But — you suspect someone?"

"At present, Mr. Withers, I'd not like to reply to that question, definitely, anyhow. What we'd like to know is — can you tell us anything?"

Mr. Withers shook his head doubtfully.

"I really don't know," he replied. "Still, there is a circumstance I must mention; indeed, it was to mention it that I came down this morning. It is this. I have, as you may be aware, acted as the late Sir John's legal adviser for some years, though, to tell you the truth, he had very seldom to have recourse to my services. Well, when I went to my office yesterday, after my many days' absence, I found a letter from Sir John, which I will now show you. You will observe that it was written from the Midland Hotel in this town and dated on the Sunday of Sir John's arrival here. Its contents surprised me — I don't know if they will occasion you any surprise or throw any light on what's happened?"

He handed over a letter, extracted from his pocketbook, and Marston and Stell read it together:

MY DEAR WITHERS, —

You will see from the heading of this where I am at present — we are here, at the Theatre Royal, for one week. I want to see you very particularly, on a matter of very serious importance. Can you run clown here, any day you like during the week? Any day you choose will suit me if you will wire me in the morning of the day you decide on that you are coming.

There are two other matters to refer to. One, will you bring my will with you? The other, I want you to bring down a thoroughly experienced chartered accountant who would be prepared to spend a few days here — or, if it is late in the week when you come, to go with me to Manchester, our next pitch.

Let me hear from you — preferably by wire.
Sincerely,
JOHN RIVERSLEY.

"There is a postscript overleaf," remarked Mr. Withers. Marston turned the sheet over.

P.S. — On second thoughts, never mind about the chartered accountant. I want the services of one at once, but there are, of course, plenty of thoroughly experienced men in this town. I want to see you first, however, before employing one. Don't forget the will. — J. R.

Marston read letter and postscript once more and handed the document back to Mr. Withers.

"What do you gather from that, sir?" he asked.

"I do not know what to make of it," replied Mr. Withers. "You see, as I said before, I know very little about Sir John Riversley's affairs. I suppose he wished for the services of a chartered accountant so that he could have something checked. His business dealings, no doubt."

"You don't know anything about his business dealings, Mr. Withers?"

"Very little. He had a very capable business manager, Mr. Carroll. But I believe that quite apart from the running of his own company, Sir John had some share in the proprietorship or managership or something of a — what do they call it? — a chain, a group, of provincial theatres. Perhaps it referred to something about that. You see, as he is dead, I am all in the dark. Of course, I have his will in my pocket, as a matter of fact."

"That's important, Mr. Withers," said Marston. "Can you — is it permissible to ask if you can tell us what the purport of the will is?"

"I see no reason why I shouldn't tell you," replied the solicitor. "It will all have to come out, now. With the exception of a trifling legacy to myself Sir John Riversley left everything he had equally divided between his manager, Carroll, and the Actor's Benevolent Fund."

"Half to Carroll, eh?" remarked Marston. "Is Carroll aware of it?"

"I don't think so. No, I'm sure he's not."

Stell interposed in the conversation — for the first time.

"How much has Sir John left?" he asked bluntly.

Mr. Withers smiled, shaking his head.

"Ah!" he replied. "Now that's a question I can't answer. I've not the faintest idea of the value of my late client's worldly estate! Not the very faintest."

"Who has?" enquired Stell.

"Well, I suppose his bankers may have," replied Mr. Withers. "He may have lodged his securities with them. He certainly never lodged them with me. Perhaps Carroll may know something."

"Carroll is still here in Hatherford," remarked Stell.

"I must see him, then," said Mr. Withers. "You see, I am in a curious position. Although I am sole executor of the will, I don't know anything about the value or character of Sir John's estate. He made money, much money, of late years, but I don't know what he did with it, nor what he was worth. He may have left fifty thousand pounds for all I know! — and again, it may be only fifty thousand pence. I haven't the least idea where his money is, nor in what his property lies. He was a reserved man in many respects — a secret man who kept things to himself."

"What about his bankers?" suggested Marston.

"Well, we can soon find out if they know anything," replied Mr. Withers. "Are you aware, gentlemen, that although Sir John Riversley left this town over twenty years ago, he still kept his banking account here? Not? — well, he did! He banked with the Hatherford Old Bank. And I think you and I, Mr. Chief Constable, had better see the manager of that bank at once."

"Yes," said Marston. "But we will take Stell with us, if you please. Stell knows all about this case so far, and must be kept posted. Shall we go now, Mr. Withers? The Hatherford Old Bank isn't five minutes away.

As a matter of strict fact, the Hatherford Old Bank was just round the corner, and within ten minutes the three men were safely closeted with its manager in his private room. He listened quietly while Mr. Withers explained the situation.

"Yes," he said when the solicitor had finished. "Sir John Riversley kept his private account here. He had kept it here from the time he left the town to go on the stage. It was a very small account at first, of course," he added with a smile. "It grew — in course of years. But what is it you want to know?"

"In a word — where my late client's securities are?" replied Withers. "They are not deposited with me. Are they deposited with you?"

"No — certainly not!" said the manager. "We have a balance, a pretty considerable balance, lying here in Sir John's favour, and we have been wondering when his executor or executors would communicate with us. But securities — no!"

"Do you know anything about his investments?" asked Mr. Withers.

"Yes — a good deal. From time to time — say two or three times a year, when there was a goodly amount of money of his in our hands — Sir John would ask us, by letter, to instruct our brokers to buy certain stock — always selected by himself — for him. We did this, of course. The usual routine, you know — he would get the contract note and a little later the stock. We never kept anything for him — contract notes and stock would be forwarded to him. Of course, we've got his receipts for the stock."

"Well, about that stock," said Mr. Withers. "What was it — inscribed, registered, or bearer?"

"Speaking from memory," replied the manager, "I think that nearly all the securities we handled for Sir John were bearer securities. For some reason he had a prejudice that way."

"Good investments?" asked Mr. Withers.

"Gilt-edged — always. He was a wise man — satisfied with four and a half per cent. All round. No risks!"

"Well, have you any idea, rough idea, of what his investments amounted to in the aggregate?"

"Again I must speak from memory. I should say twenty to twenty-five thousand pounds."

"A good deal of money! But — where are his papers? As I say, I haven't got them! And you haven't. Where are they?"

The manager smiled and spread his hands.

"Sir John Riversley had a flat in town, hadn't he?" he said. "Probably he had a safe there. Has it been examined? Has the flat been examined?"

"He had a bachelor establishment, certainly," replied Mr. Withers meditatively. "It hasn't been examined. A flat, yes — in Mount Street. Well, I suppose I must go back to town and examine everything — I've been ill, you see, or I should have done all this before."

"Oh, you'll find all his securities there!" said the manager. "As I suggested, he'll have had a safe. Of course, I only knew him by correspondence, but I should say that Sir John Riversley knew very well how to take care of anything he possessed. By the by, we only know anything of his affairs as regards his private account. Who managed his business account? — I mean, in connection with his company?"

"His business manager, Mr. Carroll. Carroll has been with him for years."

"I should suggest seeing Mr. Carroll," said the manager. "He may be able to tell you a good deal of which we are quite in ignorance."

"Carroll is here in the town, you know," remarked Marston. "Stell can show you where he's staying, Mr. Withers."

"We'll go there, then," agreed Mr. Withers. "Then I must go back to London and examine the flat. Let us see Carroll at once."

Stell conducted the solicitor in the direction of Thornholme Street. And as they turned into it they met Carroll, who was making towards the theatre. Carroll showed no surprise at seeing Mr. Withers, but he glanced at him with evident disfavour.

"I thought you'd have got here before," he said. "I wrote to you the very night of the murder. I've never heard from you!"

"I have been ill, very ill," replied Mr. Withers. "I have not been at my office for many days. When I got there yesterday, I found your letter, and also a letter from Sir John written the day before his death. Well, there are many things to clear up! I want to ask you certain questions. You know that Sir John kept his account at the Hatherford Old Bank?"

"A private account," corrected Carroll. "I know that — and that's all I know about it."

"Do you know, Carroll, where he kept his securities?"

Carroll, who had been gazing enquiringly at Stell, as if in wonder at his presence, turned an astonished look on his questioner.

"I?" he exclaimed. "Good Lord, no! I know nothing about his securities! What should I know?"

"Where he kept them, I said," repeated Mr. Withers. "You were his manager — his very confidential manager, I'm given to understand."

"In business matters," retorted Carroll. "In private matters — no! I knew nothing of his private affairs. Securities? You, or his bankers, are more likely to know about that sort of thing than I am. How should I know anything? My job was to run the business side of the company, pay out, take in, and hand over to Sir John the profits, at regular intervals. What he did with his profits was, and is, no concern of mine!"

"Did he ever have his accounts — between you and himself — audited?" asked Mr. Withers.

Carroll sneered — openly.

"What are you trying to get at?" he asked. "Yes! — if you want to know. Twice a year — and by one of the best firms of chartered accountants in the City!"

"Are you staying long in Hatherford?" asked Mr. Withers, quietly.

"Till I've finished winding things up. Done here as well as anywhere else. A few days yet, I should think."

Mr. Withers gave Carroll a cool nod and turned away.

"Let us go back to your Superintendent," he said.

He kept silence until he and Stell had once more regained Marston's room; there he flung himself into a chair and sighed deeply.

"Mr. Superintendent!" he said. "I may as well voice my thoughts. I suspect Carroll!"

Chapter 18

WHO IS CARROLL?

MARSTON was engaged in writing at his desk: he looked up with an expression of astonishment.

"Good Heavens!" he exclaimed. "You — suspect Carroll? Of what, Mr. Withers?"

"It is too soon to say that," replied the solicitor. "All I can say is — I suspect him!"

Marston looked at Stell.

"We've had no reason to suspect him," he said.

"So far!" remarked Stell.

"That may be," said Mr. Withers a little dryly. "I do!"

"But — of what?" asked Marston.

Mr. Withers put the tips of his fingers together and seemed to consider matters.

"There is something wrong," he said after a pause. "I feel there is something wrong! Intuition, if you like. But — there are certain solid grounds. Put this to yourselves. Why did Sir John Riversley ask me to come here? Why did he want me to bring his will with me? Why did he ask me to bring a chartered accountant? He had reasons for all these requests. What were they? As he's dead, he can't tell us what his reasons were. But..."

He paused again, shaking his head meaningly. After another pause Marston spoke.

"Can you suggest what they were or what you think they were?" he said. "I suppose you've some notion in your head, Mr. Withers?"

"Some!" agreed the solicitor. "As to the first question, I suppose, as I am a legal practitioner, he wished to consult me on some legal matter. As to the second, I can only suppose that as he had a copy of the will in his own possession, he wanted to destroy the original!"

"Ah, he'd a copy of the will, had he?" said Marston. "That's a point of importance. Carroll may have seen that copy!"

"As to the third," continued Mr. Withers, "I can only conclude that he wanted a chartered accountant for the purpose to which men of that calling or profession devote themselves — the examination and checking of accounts! Whose account? As far as I am aware, gentlemen, the only accounts Sir John Riversley ever had to deal with were those between himself and his business manager — Carroll!"

Once more Marston turned to Stell.

"What do we know about Carroll? — as relates to Sir John's murder?" he asked.

"Not much," replied Stell. "According to his own account, he never saw Sir John after Sir John arrived at the theatre, as he, Carroll, was at the front, with Gresford, the lessee and manager of the Theatre Royal."

"Was that corroborated?" enquired Marston.

"To this extent," answered Stell. "Gresford said that Carroll was with him, near the box office, when the news of the murder was brought to them."

"Yes — let's see, who took the news to them?"

"Pratt, Sir John's dresser. He found Sir John dead."

"You never learnt anything about Carroll's movements, or whereabouts, during the previous quarter of an hour?"

"Only from his own lips. His story was that he never saw Sir John at the theatre that evening — after Sir John came in, I mean — as he was busy checking accounts and so on at the box office. He was certainly with Gresford when Pratt sought them with the news."

Marston turned again to Mr. Withers.

"Mr. Withers," he said, "what do you know about Carroll?"

The solicitor pulled out a snuff box and helped himself to a generous pinch. "I have always considered that there was a certain amount of mystery about Carroll," he answered after a moment's reflection. "He has been Sir John's manager for some six or seven years, and he came into power in that highly important post at a very unusual age — he was, in fact, little more than a boy!"

"What do you mean by that, exactly?" asked Stell.

"Twenty or twenty-one. Sir John — who, I think, had a tendency to regard all his geese as swans — he did that, certainly, with members of his company! — used to boast about him as being an absolute financial genius. He may have been."

"Sir John had a big opinion of him, then?" suggested Marston.

"Very big! But, as I say, Sir John's tendency was to exaggerate the importance of anybody he employed. Some men are like that."

"He — Carroll — was a capable business manager, in Sir John's opinion?"

"To hear Sir John Riversley talk about him, as he did, occasionally, to me, you'd have thought that Carroll was the perfection of business managers! But, as I've twice said, that was Sir John's way. I've known him to have a perfect stick of a leading lady whom everybody loathed while he himself regarded her as a second Rachel or Bernhardt! He spoiled Carroll."

"I wish we knew more about Carroll," remarked Marston thoughtfully.

"We might know more," said Stell. "Macdermott is still in Hatherford; he's at his old lodgings. And perhaps you remember, Superintendent, what Macdermott said to you and me about Carroll when we called on Macdermott the first time?"

"No!" said Marston. "What did he say?"

"He said 'Carroll is a skunk!' Just that!"

"Then I'm afraid Macdermott could only give a prejudiced account of him," observed Marston. "Still, Macdermott has been a member of the company for some years and must know something. Couldn't you fetch him here, Stell, and — "

Mr. Withers pulled out his watch and sighed plaintively.

"I must have some food," he said. "I left London very, very early, and — "

"Step across to my club with me, sir," said Marston, rising from his desk. "We will have lunch there, at once. Stell! — you go round to Macdermott's rooms after you've had your lunch and try to get him down here. Say three o'clock."

Stell found Macdermott eating a late and solitary lunch at his old lodgings. His face lighted up as Stell entered.

"Any news?" he asked eagerly.

"Not much," replied Stell. "But — of what?"

Macdermott's face fell. He pushed away his plate.

"Oh, I meant of the poor little lady," he answered. "They promised to let me know as soon as there was any change in her condition. I suppose there isn't, yet, but I thought that you, perhaps, had heard something. What do you want with me?"

"Bit of help, Mr. Macdermott," said Stell. "Confidential — strictly private!"

"Well?" replied Macdermott. "I say neither yes nor no — till I know more."

"It's this, then," continued the detective. "Mr. Withers, Sir John Riversley's solicitor, has come down from London. He's been engaged with me and the Superintendent this morning in making some enquiries, and — now this is strictly between you and me! — he's formed some suspicions against Carroll — "

Macdermott, who was lighting a cigar, paused in the act, and cigar in one hand and match in the other, turned and stared, open-mouthed, at his visitor.

"Ah!" he said after a pause. "Carroll? Withers suspects — him? Ah! And — tell me more!"

"Not just now," replied Stell, smiling. "All in good time. Will you come to Marston's office and see him and Withers?"

"Again — what is wanted of me?" asked Macdermott.

"Information! About Carroll. You've been in the company some time, haven't you? You must know something."

"It is to be strictly confidential, young man?" enquired Macdermott. "Between me and the three of you? Very well — I'll go with you. Carroll, eh? Odd, now, but — um, I'd never thought of Carroll," he muttered, as he made for an old ulster that hung from a peg in the door. "But now I do think — um, um, um—"

"What're you mumbling to yourself?" asked Stell.

"Never mind! Queer how it is that things don't occur to one, isn't it? Now that never did occur to me!"

"What never did occur to you?" demanded Stell.

"Again I say — never mind! Come on — let us see this lawyer. No — it certainly never occurred to me — odd, very, that it shouldn't, now I come to think of it!"

"I don't know what you're talking about," said Stell.

Macdermott laughed and clapped on a hat as ancient as the ulster.

"You don't, laddie!" he answered. "You don't and you won't — yet awhile. This Withers — I've met him once or twice before — dried-up attorney, isn't he?"

"Pretty much that way," said Stell. "All there, though. And I should say that if he gets an opinion into his head it's going to stick there!"

"Right or wrong, eh?" said Macdermott. "Well — perhaps he's right, this time. But I must know what his opinions are before I contribute to any support of them, my lad! I make my entrance in silence — see?"

Marston and Mr. Withers made their entrance in company with Alderman Wardle, whom they had met at the Club. Mr. Withers, in spite of his ascetic appearance, had lunched well, and was indisposed to talk, and at his invitation, and it being understood that everything was — as Alderman Wardle said — sub rosa, he repeated to Macdermott and Wardle all that he had said to Marston and Stell.

"And what we want to know from you, Mr. Macdermott — whom I now recognise as having met before —" he concluded, "is — what can you tell us about Carroll? You have been a prominent member of the late Sir John Riversley's company for some years and should know a good deal. Now, again — what can you tell us?"

Macdermott threw away the end of his cigar — and took one which Wardle offered him out of a well-filled case.

"What do you want to know, Mr. Withers?" he asked.

"Well, perhaps I can put the question into these words," replied Mr. Withers. "These! — who is Carroll?"

Macdermott smoked for a minute or two in silence.

"Aye, well," he replied at last. "I've heard two or three things said on that point, in the company, at one time or another. Some of the folk I've worked with for Sir John Riversley have said that Carroll is his son!"

"Ah!" exclaimed Mr. Withers. "Son?"

"Others have said that Carroll is his nephew."

"Nephew?"

"And others, again, have said that Carroll is the orphan child of a deceased actor for whom Sir John had a great affection..."

"Aye, aye?" interrupted Mr. Withers eagerly, "and..."

"And to wind up with, I've heard it said that Carroll is the son of a noted lady for whom Sir John once had a great weakness," concluded Macdermott. "As for myself, I don't know who Carroll is! And I don't believe he knows himself."

"When did you first know or have knowledge of Carroll, Mr. Macdermott?"

"About seven years ago, Mr. Withers — when the Sir John Riversley company was first formed. For the first year, Sir John had as business manager a man named Corfield, but it was well known that he was nothing but a warming-pan for somebody who was coming. The somebody was Carroll. Sir John used to talk about him. He used to tell us that he'd a smart young fellow, a young friend of his, in prospect for the managership as soon as he left Cambridge — "

"Oh, Carroll was at Cambridge, was he?" asked Marston.

"Sure, he's a varsity man," replied Macdermott, "and had all the side and swank of these fellows when he came to us. Well, he came, and I'll say this for him, that he took to his job in an extraordinarily clever fashion. Corfield stayed on a bit, to show him the way of it, but he very soon knew more than Corfield would ever have known. He's a damn sharp fellow, Carroll!"

"A really good business manager, eh?" asked Wardle. "Sound?"

"Good as could be, and sound as can be, sir — in his employer's interests," replied Macdermott. "Arithmetic, mathematics, and them sort of things I was never good at myself, and 'tis the very haziest ideas I have of what is called accountancy, but Carroll 'ud beat all the Senior Wranglers ever was produced with Euclid and Barnard Smith thrown in!"

"Very good hand at figures, eh?" asked Marston, with a wink at Stell and Wardle.

"The best! His books hadn't a scratch or a blot in 'em!"

"Might be good at manipulating figures, too," said Marston aside. "Well, Mr. Macdermott, if Mr. Withers has done with you, there's a question or two I'd like to ask. Were Sir John and his business manager on good terms?"

"They were inseparable," replied Macdermott. "I told you that some of the company used to hint that they were father and son. They were always together — as a rule they stayed together at hotels. Now 'tis a queer circumstance, but this Hatherford was the very first place I ever remember them not staying together! Sir John was at the Midland Hotel; Carroll went to where he now is, Mrs. Milford's, just above where I myself am staying, at Mrs. Smith's. Unusual — very unusual! It means something — a quarrel, or something of that sort."

"Do you know of any quarrel — just before they came to Hatherford?"

"I do not, for I had one of my own with Jack Riversley that was occupying my attention. You see — "

A policeman knocked; entered.

"Mr. Pratt wishes to see you, sir," he announced. "Or he'd see Mr. Stell if it's not convenient for you — "

"Pratt? That's Sir John's dresser," said Marston. "Bring him in, Smith. Now what can Pratt want? If he's anything to tell..."

Chapter 19

THE BLACK DESPATCH BOX

IT was quite obvious that if Pratt had a tale to tell it was one the weight of which was resting heavily on his mind: Pratt looked miserable and unhappy. He responded silently to Marston's greeting, and taking the chair which Stell placed for him, groaned aloud.

"What's the matter, Pratt?" asked the Superintendent. "Something wrong?"

Pratt drew out a pocket handkerchief and wiped away a tear.

"Seems to me that everything's gone wrong since — since that happened, sir," he replied. "And I've got that muddled that I scarcely know what I'm doing at times! But in this matter that I've come to see you about — the fact is, sir, there's a piece of my late poor master's property missing."

"Yes?" responded Marston. "What, now?"

"Never struck me about it till this very morning, sir," continued Pratt. "I've been that bothered, getting and collecting Sir John's things, at the hotel, and at the theatre, and one thing and another, that — well, it's just this, sir. My master had a black morocco despatch box — a very expensive article, sir, with a patent lock — which he always carried with him everywhere. He was never parted from it, sir. Used to stand on his table wherever he stayed, and on his bedside table at night, and was always taken by him, himself, to the various theatres. What you'd call inseparables, Sir John and that despatch box. Well, sir, I can't find it!"

"Where have you looked for it?" asked Stell.

"There's only one place where I could look for it, Mr. Stell," replied Pratt. "The dressing room!"

"Yes, but how can you be sure that he took it there on that particular evening?" asked Stell. "For once, he may have left it at the hotel."

"No, sir! He wouldn't — and I know he didn't."

"How do you know that, now?"

"Because I've been up to the theatre and seen Jenkinson, the stage doorkeeper, Mr. Stell. Jenkinson remembers quite well that Sir John was carrying the black despatch case when he passed in."

"How is it you never thought of this before, my lad?" enquired Wardle. "You've had several days to clear things up in."

"I'm aware of it, sir," admitted Pratt. "But what with one thing and another, it clean slipped my memory. You see, sir, there was my poor master's wardrobe at the theatre — quite a serious thing to pack, sir — dresses for his various parts. And there were his things at the hotel — six or seven trunks, sir. Sir John, gentlemen, was what you'd call a dressy gentleman — he'd always twelve or fifteen different suits of clothes with him. I've had a deal to do, gentlemen."

"Have you enquired at the theatre, Pratt?" asked Marston.

"Oh, yes, high and low. I can't find anybody that ever set eyes on the despatch box, except, as I said, Jenkinson. And that was when Sir John entered."

"Let's see," said Marston. "It was you, Pratt, who discovered Sir John's dead body, wasn't it?"

"It was, sir — it was, indeed!"

"Did you see the despatch case then?"

"I can't say that I did, sir. And again I can't say that I didn't. If it was there then, I never noticed it."

"You ran straight off to give the alarm, I suppose?"

"Yes, sir. I ran to find Mr. Carroll."

"Just so! To be sure, Mr. Carroll. Now where did you find Mr. Carroll?"

"Talking to Mr. Gresford, sir, just by the box office."

"Did you notice anybody else about there?"

"Not particularly, sir. I was excited and upset."

"Do you know, or did you know, that young man Clegg who died under mysterious circumstances the other night?"

"I did, sir. Not then, though — at least, not to know his name. I knew him by sight as one of the young gentlemen in the office, sir. I got to know his name afterwards."

"Did you see Clegg anywhere about when you spoke to Carroll and Gresford?"

"Not then, sir. But I had just seen him."

"You had just seen him? Where, Pratt?"

"In the passage that led from the downstairs dressing rooms to the front of the theatre, sir. He was standing in that passage with some books and papers under his arm. I spoke to him — he was the first I spoke to."

"What did you say to him, Pratt?"

"I said 'Where's Mr. Carroll — where's Mr. Carroll?' That was all, sir — I was running along the passage."

"What did he reply?"

"I don't know what he replied, sir. I think he said 'What's the matter?' or something of that sort — I didn't wait to hear. I knew where Mr. Carroll was likely to be, you see, sir."

"Mr. Carroll went straight back to the dressing room with you, didn't he?"

"Yes, sir — he and Mr. Gresford."

"Was Clegg still in that passage?"

"I didn't see him, sir. But I was too upset, knocked clean over, to be in any condition to notice things."

"I understand," said Marston. "Well, Pratt, Mr. Stell will make some enquiries. In the meantime don't say anything about this missing despatch box. Have you mentioned the matter to anyone?"

"Oh, yes, sir. Mr. Carroll, of course. He's made enquiry at the theatre. But he's not heard anything of it."

"Well, don't tell anybody else," said Marston. "What are you doing, Pratt? — staying here?"

"I'm under Mr. Carroll's orders, sir. Everything's packed up, now. I'm waiting to know what Mr. Carroll tells me to do."

"Very well, Pratt. But let us know what your movements are. Don't go away without seeing me."

Pratt left — and Marston turned to Mr. Withers.

"Have you ever seen the black morocco despatch case he spoke of?" he asked.

"Yes!" replied Withers. "Often! Sir John always had it with him whenever he called at my office."

"You go and make some enquiry about it at the theatre, Stell," said Marston. "Find out, if you can, if Sir John really did take it with him from the hotel that evening." He turned again to Mr. Withers. "There's just one more matter I'd like cleared up — if you can throw any light on it. There seems to have been some very close kinship, relationship, or whatever you like to call it, between Sir John Riversley and Carroll. Now, Mr. Macdermott says that Carroll came straight from college to be Sir John's manager. Does anyone — do you, Mr. Withers? Do you, Mr. Macdermott? — know anything of Carroll's life before that?"

"I don't!" replied Mr. Withers.

"I do!" said Macdermott. "Riversley educated him. He was at Abbotshampton — and that's a grand enough establishment, you'll admit. I went there once, with Riversley, to see the young fellow."

"You did?" asked Marston.

"I did so! I was a great pal of Jack Riversley's at that time."

"Who did Riversley say the lad was, then?"

"Oh, he told me he was the son of old friends of his — sort of ward. I didn't believe him. I don't know what I thought. As I told you before, there were all sorts of things said in the company when young Carroll finally came and took hold of the business — that he was Riversley's son; that he was his nephew; and so on and so on. I never said he was anything: I just endured him!"

"You don't like the man, Mr. Macdermott?" suggested Wardle.

"Carroll, sir, is a skunk!" said Macderrnott. "I have no more to say."

"I think no one has any more to say — at present," said Marston. "And let us keep what's been said to ourselves. Mr. Withers, you'll be staying here for a day or two, anyway? Let me know where. The Midland Hotel? — all right, sir. Stell — go and make these enquiries at the theatre."

Stell went off there and then. He found Jenkinson in his little snug just within the stage door. Jenkinson, known to Stell pretty intimately, was a sociable and talkative fellow. Stell, instead of plunging into the middle of things, passed the time of day with him and at first talked of nothing particular. But Jenkinson brought the conversation round to the murder.

"Getting on at all?" he asked meaningly. "Anything new?"

"Not much," replied Stell almost indifferently. "Difficult case."

"Think that affair of young Clegg's had any relation to the other business?" enquired Jenkinson. "Sprung out of it, as it were?"

"May have done," said Stell. "That's, perhaps, a queerer business than the first! What's being said about it here, Jack?"

Jenkinson laughed — satirically.

"Why, what do you expect would be said?" he answered. "You're a nice detective, aren't you? There's only one thing could be said, is there? And everybody's saying it."

"Well?" asked Stell, imperturbable as ever. "And what's that?"

"Why, that Clegg knew — something! And about — somebody. And that that somebody carefully put him — where all is silence! Natural conclusion to draw, isn't it, my boy?"

"S'pose so," assented Stell. He remained leaning over the ledge of Jenkinson's little window, staring at the photographs of stage celebrities with which the doorkeeper's sanctum was liberally decorated. "You remember Sir John coming in that night, I suppose?" he said suddenly.

"I do!" replied Jenkinson. "Uncommon well!"

"Do you remember if he was carrying anything?"

"Aye, I remember that! A black morocco despatch box, or case — a very swell article. Name — his name — on it, in gold letters."

"You seem to have taken particular notice of it!"

"Couldn't miss doing so. He stopped to talk to me a minute or two when he came in, and he set the case down on that ledge, where you've got your elbow at this minute. Oh, yes, I remember it. And what about it?"

"Between you and me, Jack," said Stell, "it's missing! Been missing ever since — well, I should say ever since you saw it. I should think you were the last person to see it — except himself and the individual who stole it."

"Murderer, eh?" suggested Jenkinson.

"Likely! Anyhow, Sir John took it into his dressing room, didn't he?"

"He took it away in his hand from that ledge, certainly. Yes, of course, he'd take it into his dressing room."

"Well — it's missing, I tell you. But keep that to yourself. Now I want to see Mr. Gresford."

Stell found the manager in his private office, very busy with a secretary. But he sent the secretary away and shut the door on the detective and himself.

"Want to know something, Stell?" he asked abruptly.

"Yes," replied Stell with equal directness. "I want to know if you've got a pretty clear recollection of what happened that night of Sir John Riversley's murder?"

"I think so," said Gresford. "I remember that clearly enough, anyway!"

"I want you to try and recall things that happened, or things as they were, during the half hour before you heard of the murder," continued Stell. "Where were you between six-fifteen and six-forty-five?"

"Where I always am at that time. At the front — somewhere about the box office. Seeing after things, you know."

"Was Carroll with you all that time?"

Gresford thought awhile.

"Not all the time. I remember seeing him at about a quarter-past six, and then again later. I remember seeing him in the box office, checking some figures or looking over the bookings. He was with me, near the box office, when the news of the murder was brought to us."

"But he hadn't been with you continuously?"

"Not continuously, certainly. I — well, kept seeing him about."

"There may have been times, a time, when you didn't see him?"

"Oh, yes. Probably ten minutes or so."

"Well, another question," said Stell.

"This is about Clegg. He was employed in the box office, wasn't he?"

"Clerk — yes."

"Did you call or fetch him out of the box office that evening to go anywhere?"

"Yes! I called him out and sent him to Jenkinson, at the stage door, to see if some account books and papers had been left there — things that I wanted."

"Would he have to pass the door of Sir John's dressing room, going and returning?"

"He would! What's it all about, Stell? Any suspicion — "

Stell rose from his chair.

"I'd rather not say at present," he replied. "You'll know all in due course."

He went away from the theatre and returned slowly to the City Hall. Marston was not in his room. As he came away from it a constable came up to him.

"The Super left a message for you, sergeant," he said. "He's gone over to the Hyacinth Club with Alderman Wardle. He said would you join them as soon as ever you came in?"

Chapter 20

THE SIGNIFICANT REMARK

STELL found Marston in a corner of the smoking room at the Hyacinth Club; he sat behind a round table, with Mr. Withers on one hand and Alderman Wardle on the other. And on the table before them lay a pink, flimsy sheet of paper — the paper on which telegrams are sent out in England. Marston picked it up as Stell approached and handed it to him as he took a seat.

"Read that, Stell," he said. "Another surprise!"

Stell bent over the telegram. He noted at once that it had been despatched from Barcelona, in Spain, and that it was addressed to the Superintendent of Police at Hatherford.

Can give some important information concerning Sir John Riversley am leaving here via Paris tonight will see you on arrival in meantime see the Mayor. Braithwaite.

Stell knew who Braithwaite was — one of the most prominent solicitors in the town. But — Barcelona?

"I didn't know Mr. Braithwaite was in Spain," he remarked as he placed the telegram on the table.

"I did," said Wardle. "He's gone over there on behalf of Felstead, Parkholme & Co., of Hatherdale Mills. They've got some important law business on with a Spanish firm at Barcelona. Braithwaite went off on the very day Sir John Riversley was murdered — that night, in fact. He was at the lunch that the Mayor gave to Sir John — he told me then that he was setting out for Spain that evening."

"What's this mean about seeing the Mayor?" asked Stell.

"We shall soon know," said Marston. "I've been on the phone with his Worship; he's coming across here, presently."

Wardle picked up his glass and took a drink.

"It's a queer business, this!" he remarked. "Gets queerer and queerer. Anything been heard about Mrs. Wollaton?"

"She's in just about the same state," replied Marston. "Quiescent. Memory still — just as it was. I've spoken to two or three of our medical men about it — they say she may recover it all of a sudden. Dr. Phipps, now, he told me only this morning that a sudden shock might bring it back. But then, what sort of a shock? You can't go on submitting a delicate, nervous woman to a series of shocks!"

"I reckon that what he meant was that she lost her memory through a shock, and that it might be returned by a similar shock," suggested Wardle. "But what was the shock that upset her?"

"I don't think there is much doubt about it, sir," said Stell. "It was something she saw, or that happened, in that dressing room."

"Aye!" said Wardle. "Just so! I've no doubt she could tell a good deal, poor lady, if she could only speak. Well, as I said just now, it gets queerer and queerer. Telegrams from Barcelona now. And this uncertainty as to where Sir John kept his money

— his securities. And this Clegg affair — anything more heard about that, Superintendent?"

"I've heard something," replied Marston. "I got the report of the postmortem examination of Clegg just before coming across here. The doctors say, definitely, that he was poisoned."

"That's established, is it?" asked Wardle. "No doubt, eh?"

"There's no doubt. He was poisoned! — that's that. The doctors think he'd had some poison — they're not exactly certain what, yet, till there's been an analysis — administered to him not very long before he dropped in the street. But you know, up to now, we can't get any information as to Clegg's movements that night. We know that he called at Mrs. Milford's for a few minutes, but that's all. And that was some time before he collapsed opposite the chemist's shop."

"Let's see — doesn't Carroll lodge at Mrs. Milford's?" asked Wardle.

"He does — but Carroll wasn't in when Clegg called there. That was why he didn't stay long. He went off — but where to? We can't get a scrap of information about his subsequent movements!"

"Here's the Mayor!" said Stell.

The others turned towards the door, where a pageboy was showing in a little, active, consequential-looking man of middle age whose slightly raised head, sharp eyes, and pointed red beard gave an impression of restless energy. This was the Worshipful the Mayor of Hatherford — in private life Mr. Thomas Wingham, a highly successful tradesman who had reached the highest honours his native town could give him at a comparatively early age, and was fully conscious of his own power and importance. This was his second year of office, and he had almost forgotten what it was to pin an apron round him and serve behind the counter of his grocery establishment — a palatial one — in Market Street. While he was Mayor, Mr. Thomas Wingham said, he was Mayor, and nothing else but Mayor; whoever visited him must seek him not at Wingham Brothers, grocers and Italian warehousemen, but in the Mayor's Parlour at the City Hall. It was there that Marston had rung him up.

The Mayor came bustling forward — he reminded most people of a turkey-cock when it struts, tail spread, across a farmyard — bestowing nods to one and another of the four men at the table and rubbing his hands together as if in the act of washing them.

"How do, Alderman? — how do, Super? — how do, sergeant? — and this gentleman, eh? — friend of somebody's, eh?" he said. "Came across to talk here, Marston — so many interruptions across there, you know. Got a few minutes only — what is it, now?"

"Mr. Mayor," said Marston, "this gentleman is Mr. Withers, from London, solicitor to the late Sir John Riversley. Mr. Withers has come down — "

"To make enquiries, of course," interrupted the Mayor. "Very natural — very proper! How do you do, sir — hope I see you well? Very queer case this, Mr. Withers — uncommon queer case. Perhaps you can throw some light on it, sir?"

Before Mr. Withers could speak, Marston picked up Braithwaite's telegram.

"There's something here, Mr. Mayor, on which you can throw light," he said. "This is a telegram from Mr. Braithwaite, who's at Barcelona — "

"Aye, I know — gone over on that Felstead business," said the Mayor. "Well?"

"Mr. Braithwaite — but read the telegram for yourself," continued Marston. "You'll see that Mr. Braithwaite says that he can give some information on this matter of Sir John Riversley's death when he returns, and that in the meantime I'm to see you. That's why I phoned you."

The Mayor took the telegram, put on a pair of gold pince-nez, and made a careful inspection of the message. Then he laid the telegram down, took off his glasses, and looked round, as if in search of something.

"Um!" he said. "Ah! Well, so there's a bit of talking to be done, and as talking's dry work, I'll take a whisky-and-soda with you, Wardle. Um!" he continued as Wardle beckoned a waiter and gave him a whispered order, " it's just this, gentlemen — I can guess what Braithwaite means, and I can tell you something, but what it has, or whether it has, to do with the murder of Sir John Riversley I can't tell you, for I don't know! If I'd ever thought it had, I should, of course, have mentioned it before. But here it is! You know that when Sir John came to play here, I, knowing he was a native, asked him, I being the Mayor, to a luncheon party at the City Hall? Well, on the Monday morning I got a note from him, delivered at the Mayor's Parlour. It was what I call a queer sort of note. Not the first part of it — that was all right; just a polite acceptance of my invitation, d'ye see? But then it went off on to another thing. He wanted to know if I could call on him at the Midland Hotel some time that morning, and if I could, would I bring a solicitor with me, who must be a man of the first standing in the legal profession. Well, I thought that a very strange request, but then, as we all know, these actors and actresses are strange people. So I sent back a reply that I'd wait on him in an hour's time and bring a gentleman with me who would no doubt satisfy his requirements. And in due course I went across to the Midland and took Braithwaite."

The waiter returned with the Mayor's whisky-and-soda, and the Mayor paused to refresh himself, and to wish his companions the best of health. Setting his glass down, he resumed his story with obvious relish of the telling of it.

"Well, as I say, Braithwaite and I went there, neither of us knowing what he wanted with us. He was very grand, very much the fine gentleman — might have been a Duke! I reckon these play-acting chaps pretend to be lords and princes and suchlike till they really believe they are! Of course we must have a glass of wine with him, and he ordered in a big bottle of champagne — this was all in his private sitting room, you understand. Cigars, too — he knew how to do things, I assure you. Well, after a bit of general talk, he got down to business. And what do you think it was? Of course, you've no idea. He told me, with a lot of what I should call sentimental stuff, that he was a lone man; had never married, and never should; had neither kin nor kith in the world, and nothing to lavish his affection on but his native town, and having been much impressed by it since his arrival the previous day had decided to leave it all his fortune! Just that, gentlemen! — and he added to that announcement, in his best style, these very words, 'The whole of my fortune, gentlemen — and not an inconsiderable one!'"

"Was that what he wanted Mr. Braithwaite for?" asked Mr. Withers quietly.

"You've hit it, sir!" replied the Mayor. "Sir John wanted to make a new will, leaving all his money to this town of Hatherford, and what he wanted Braithwaite and myself for was to hear from us what we could advise him as to the most fitting objects of his benevolence — hospitals, infirmaries, almshouses, charities and the like. He told me that he had a will in existence, in the hands of his solicitors — that's you, I suppose, sir?"

"That's me," assented Mr. Withers.

"But that he'd sent for you, and for the will, and that he intended to destroy it, and that afterwards he invited you and Mr. Braithwaite, between you, to draw up a new will. And when he'd told us this, gentlemen, he made what I now consider a very significant remark. It was this: 'I have been deceived, gentlemen,' he said, 'deceived by one upon whom I have lavished favours!' Then he spouted something — poetry, I think it was, Shakespeare, Braithwaite said — about nursing vipers in one's bosom. What it really came to, in plain words, that in his first will he'd left money to somebody who'd subsequently deceived him, some way, and — "

"He didn't mention any name?" asked Marston.

"He didn't — not a name. Just that. Well, I'd an important engagement, and I had to go. I left Braithwaite there to talk further to him. And that's all I know, except that he came to my luncheon party in his honour — you saw him there, you, too, Marston and Wardle. So, of course, it's all I can tell you. I don't know what he did with Braithwaite, for I never saw Braithwaite to talk to again — he went off to Barcelona that evening. And now," concluded the Mayor, picking up his glass again, "do you think all that's anything to do with Sir John's murder?"

None of the four men at whom the Mayor glanced interrogatively spoke. Three of them showed no disposition to do so. But after a while, Wardle, who knew least of the three, found his tongue.

"What I should like to know," he said oracularly, "and it seems to me a matter of great importance in this — who's the individual that Sir John Riversley referred to as a viper that he'd warmed in his bosom? Tell me that!"

"And supposing you were told, Alderman?" asked the Mayor.

"I should say then — see to that man! For you look here," continued Wardle, growing more and more judicial, "supposing that man, the viper, as we'll call him, knew that Sir John had named him in his will — a not unlikely thing — and supposing he knew that his conduct had been such as to make Sir John cut him out of his will, wouldn't that be an incentive to him to get rid of Sir John before Sir John could do the cutting out? What d'ye make of that, now?"

"There's something in that, Alderman," agreed the Mayor. "Yes, there's a good deal in that! But that would argue that the viper, as we'll call him, was in very close touch with Sir John."

"That," replied Wardle magisterially, "that, Mr. Mayor, goes without saying. I should say in the closest touch."

"What's Marston say?" asked the Mayor, "and what's this young man say?" — pointing to Stell. "They're in the know!"

"I should prefer to say nothing, at present," said Marston. "Much obliged to your Worship for coming over, all the same. I think our best plan is to await Mr. Braithwaite's arrival. He remained with Sir John when your Worship left — therefore he may have more to tell."

"Oh, no doubt, no doubt!" agreed the Mayor. He drank off his whisky-and-soda, looked at his watch, and got up. "I must be off," he said. "Committee meeting in an hour and I haven't had my bit of dinner yet. Well, keep your nose to the scent, Marston — it's a disgrace to the town to have a murder in it and not bring the murderer to justice."

He bustled away then, and presently Wardle followed him. Stell left, too, leaving Marston and Mr. Withers together. Once outside the Club Stell hesitated awhile, as if debating something within himself. Eventually he set off across the town and made for the Hunter's Horn. There, in their favourite corner, he found Clifton Claye and Bateson.

Chapter 21

SIMPSON'S YARD

THE old actor greeted Stell with a cry of approving welcome and made a place for him at his side. "Hello, young Vidocq!" he exclaimed. "Come your ways in, and sit by the old man, laddie! We were just talking about you."

"What about me?" asked Stell, dropping into the proffered seat. "Nothing good, I reckon!"

"Neither good nor bad, laddie! We were wondering — at least I was, for Bateson there is one of those cynical people who never wonder about anything — how you were getting on with your case? Now, how are things?"

"Not so satisfactory as they might be," replied Stell.

"All the more reason why you should be comforted with a drink," said Claye, turning to the barmaid. "Here, miss! — Mr. Stell's usual. And Mr. Bateson and myself will have another. I pay — I pay! — I'm still in funds, thanks to good old Mac."

"Have you seen Macdermott, Clifton?" asked Stell.

"I've seen Mac twice, laddie — he's been to see me twice, has Mac, like the good man he is. But Mac's in the melancholy mood — soon depressed, laddie!"

"What about?" demanded Stell.

"Well, well, I don't know that there's any great secret about it, laddie. This poor lady — you know who I mean. Mac has the complaint that affects all of our profession — he's sentimental. Sentimental, very sentimental, is Mac!"

"Fat lot of good that does!" growled Bateson. "Rubbish!"

"You're a cynic, Bateson," said the old actor. "A cynic! Ah, my boy, don't you despise sentiment! Sentiment, laddie, is — ah, well, never mind! You're a good fellow, Bateson, and a very fair critic, but you're too material, my dear lad, too material, and you wouldn't understand me if I told you what sentiment is. Too fine a flower for you, Bateson! And what news is there, young Stell? — must be some, surely!"

"No news for either retail or wholesale purposes," replied Stell. "Sealed lips, you know!"

"I see, I see! Know something but not going to say what, eh? Very proper, of course. Still we can all help a bit, laddie. 'In the multitude of councillors,' you know — I fancy that's in the old Book, isn't it? Suggestion — even from a mere worm like poor old Clifton Claye — has its values, laddie."

"Well, what does Clifton Claye suggest, then?" asked Stell, good-humouredly. "Always open to suggestions at our shop!"

"Clifton Claye, laddie, suggests that somewhere in this town of Hatherford Jack Riversley had a secret enemy," replied the old actor. "And a damned clever one! There! — that represents the strength of my convictions. I don't think I've ever said 'damn' for twenty years, and I mustn't say it again, you know."

"Time you did, then!" said Bateson with a laugh. "But I reckon you're afraid of being damned if you do, Clifton!"

"Clifton's afraid of nothing, my lad," declared the old man, thumping his stick on the floor. "He has his record! But joking apart, Stell, my laddie, that's my theory. And I know others who hold it. Secret! A secret enemy! Delve deep, my boy; delve deep in the matter. For you've got to deal with somebody who's — "

"Damned clever!" sneered Bateson.

"Devilish clever, anyhow," concluded Clifton Claye. "And who knows how to keep in those shades of darkness from which he emerged to accomplish his bloody purpose! How does that strike you, young Stell?"

"It would strike me a lot more if I knew who you had in mind!" said Stell. "Give him a name!"

"His name is Nemo — as far as I'm concerned, laddie!" said Claye. "He's nobody, and somebody!" He thumped the floor again with his stick and rose to his feet. "But I'm somebody too," he continued, "and I have a landlady — in short, Mrs. McGilligan — and if I'm not home to my bit of warm supper to the minute I shall hear that good lady's eloquence — good night, laddies."

The old man stumped his way out and Bateson turned to Stell.

"Glad you've come in," he said, "I was going to find you tonight."

"You?" said Stell. "Why?"

Bateson glanced round. The barmaid had retired to a seat near the fire and there was no one else in the room, but he lowered his voice.

"I've heard something," he said. "Something you ought to know. About Clegg!"

Stell turned sharply.

"What about — him?" he asked.

Bateson edged himself a little nearer to the detective.

"Listen!" he said in a still lower voice. "There was a man in the *Observer* office came to me this afternoon — a chap named Trubshaw, who's in the machine department. He asked me if I didn't know you pretty well. I said, of course, that I did and asked him why? He said that he could give some information about Clegg's movements on the evening of his death, and wouldn't mind doing so, if he could be assured that it would all be confidential; he didn't want, he said, to be dragged into it — at least, unless it was absolutely necessary in the interests of justice."

"What is it he can tell?" enquired Stell.

"Ah, that I don't know — he wouldn't tell me," replied Bateson. "But he did say this much — that it wasn't very much he could tell, but what he could tell would probably give you a clue. Just that!"

"That's a good deal," replied Stell. "When can I see this man? And where?"

Bateson glanced at his watch.

"We could see him about now," he replied. "He'll not be busy for a good hour, and I could get him out for ten minutes or so. I'll tell you what we'll do. Let's walk down to the Woolpack Inn, in Churchgate — that's just behind the Observer office, and I'll fetch him out and bring him to you there. That's about as quiet a place as I know — nothing doing there much of an evening."

Stell nodded his acquiescence, and the two men set out and went down town to the narrow street in its centre which Bateson had mentioned. Halfway down it stood the Woolpack, one of the oldest taverns in Hatherlord. Its ground floor possessed a series of small parlours — called "snugs" in those parts — and after looking into one and another of them Stell settled himself in an unoccupied one and Bateson went away to fetch his man. In five minutes he was back with him, and Bateson, after ordering drinks and ensuring their immediate supply, shut the door of the parlour upon the three of them.

Stell, meanwhile, had been subjecting Trubshaw to a critical inspection, and had decided that he was a man whose word could be trusted. Trubshaw was a little, quick-eyed man, a typical Hatherford artisan, whose alertness of manner was not incompatible with marked signs of reserve and caution: Stell saw at once that he was the sort of man who is not averse to telling what he knows if he is certain that he will do no harm to himself by telling it.

"Mr. Bateson says there's something you can tell me," said Stell suddenly, "about Clegg!"

Trubshaw pursed up his lips and nodded. He, too, on his part, had been inspecting Stell. His lips relaxed.

"Well, there is something I can tell, Mr. Stell," he answered. "But I should like my name kept out of it, d'ye see? I have to live with my neighbours, Mr. Stell, like the rest of us, I suppose, and very likely what I can tell you may affect one or other of 'em. I can't say about that."

"You don't know anything that would affect any person you can put a name to?" asked Stell.

"I don't, sir! All I can tell is something about Clegg himself."

"Then you need have no fear," said Stell. "You're not going to mention any names, except his. And he's dead. Now what about him?"

"Well, just this, Mr. Stell. You know that you people have been asking for information about Clegg's movements that night he died in the street? I understand you haven't got much?"

"Very little!"

"I can give you a bit. Do you know Simpson's Yard, Mr. Stell?"

"I don't — not even by name."

"Simpson's Yard — perhaps Mr. Bateson knows it — is at the side of the Theatre Royal; leastways, you get to it by the street that runs down the side of the theatre not the street where the stage door is, but the street on the other side. You get into Simpson's Yard by a passageway out of that street; left-hand side going down. It's a very old bit of the town, Simpson's Yard. There's about eight or ten cottages in it. I live in one of 'em."

"Yes," said Stell.

"Well, Mr. Stell, on that night we're talking about, I was taken a bit poorly at the office — Observer, you know — and I had to go home. As I turned into the passage I've just mentioned, that leads into Simpson's Yard, Clegg came out of it — nearly ran into me. We said a good night to each other; he went up the street, and I went into the yard and home. That's all!"

"Scarcely!" said Stell. "There's a lot yet. You knew Clegg?"

"Well enough by sight, Mr. Stell. I knew his name, too, and what he was — a clerk at the Theatre Royal."

"You weren't mistaken? — you're sure it was Clegg that you met?"

"Take my solemn oath and 'davy of it, sir. It was Clegg!"

"Well, and what time was it when you met him? That's highly important."

"I know it is, Mr. Stell, but I can fix it. When I heard the news next morning — of his being seen to drop in the street and so on, I let my mind go back to our meeting of the previous night. On comparing the time that he was seen to collapse opposite that chemist's shop with the time of my entering my own cottage, I made out that he died within ten minutes of leaving me."

"How long would it take him to walk from Simpson's Yard — the entrance, where you met him — to the place where he collapsed?" asked Stell.

"You can ascertain that very easily for yourself, sir," replied Trubshaw. "I should say six or seven minutes."

"Ordinary pace, or sharp walking?"

"Well, sharpish walking."

"Was Clegg walking sharply when you saw him?"

"He went up the street at a good pace, yes."

"Had you ever seen him in or near Simpson's Yard before?"

"No, never!"

"Have you any idea, Trubshaw, about his being there that night?"

Trubshaw shook his head.

"Now that's just what I did not want to be drawn into, Mr. Stell!" he said regretfully. "I didn't want to mention any names!"

"Between ourselves, you know!" said Stell.

"Well, an idea certainly did occur to me. You see, Clegg was employed at the theatre. Well, we've another employee of the theatre living in our yard."

"Yes? Who?"

Trubshaw looked from one man to the other.

"Mrs. Ubbard!" he answered.

Stell stared his sudden surprise.

"Mrs. Ubbard?" he said. "The old charwoman?"

"That's it, sir," replied Trubshaw. "Lives in the far corner of our yard, Mrs. Ubbard — or as everybody calls her, Mother Ubbard — does."

"And you thought Clegg might have been to see her?"

"I thought he might have been with a message to her."

Stell thought awhile, looking speculatively at Trubshaw.

"I suppose you couldn't find out — somehow — if Clegg had been to Mrs. Ubbard's?" he suggested. "Neighbours, eh?"

"I don't want any of our neighbours to know that I ever saw Clegg in our quarters!" declared Trubshaw. "No, sir, I can't find out."

Again Stell thought awhile.

"What sort of woman is Mrs. Ubbard?" he asked suddenly.

Trubshaw smiled.

"Queer!" he answered. "A bit — eh?" He tapped his forehead significantly. "Seen better days, I believe," he added.

Presently Trubshaw went away, and Stell and Bateson walked out into the street.

"You were asking about Mrs. Ubbard," said Bateson. "I wasn't going to say before Trubshaw, but I know something about her. You'd never think it, but that ugly old harridan was once a pretty well-known actress! Fact, my lad! Many and many a long year ago, though. What brought her to this? Pooh! — drink! Gin, my lad, gin — and plenty of it."

He went off, laughing cynically, and Stell, suddenly remembering that he had not yet been home to his supper, turned in that direction. He had to pass the Theatre Royal on his way, and at the end of the next street remembered Simpson's Yard, and turned down to it. A woman was coming out of the passage entrance, and he stopped and spoke to her.

"Can you tell me where Mrs. Ubbard lives?" he asked.

The woman answered readily, turning and pointing.

"It's the house in that left-hand corner, mister," she said. "But Mrs. Ubbard's not in. She's gone away."

Chapter 22

THE LOCKED HOUSE

STELL made some acknowledgment of this answer and turned to go, but suddenly pausing he looked more closely at his informant. She was a middle-aged, respectable-looking woman...

"How do you know Mrs. Ubbard's gone away?" he asked suddenly.

The woman looked at him.

"Why," she replied, "I conclude she's gone away because I haven't seen her about these last few days!" Then eyeing him again, she said, "Aren't you Mr. Stell, the detective?"

"Well, I am, missus," admitted Stell. "Why do you ask?"

"I saw you at the inquest on the actor gentleman," she answered. "Me and a neighbour of mine went to it — you see, the theatre's so near that we have a sort of interest in it. Mrs. Ubbard, now, she worked at the theatre, Mr. Stell."

"I know," said Stell. "Look here — when did you see Mrs. Ubbard last?"

"When did I see her last? Well, now, it would be some evenings since. I went into her house to borrow a loaf of bread

— my husband, he'd brought a friend in for a bit of supper and I was short."

"Did she say anything to you about going away?" asked Stell.

"She didn't, Mr. Stell. I didn't stop a minute. She'd a young man there — "

"A young man there?"

"Yes, a young man — I took him for one of those chaps that come after insurance money, or rates, or something of that sort — he was writing something in a little book when I went in."

"You didn't know him?"

"Me? I didn't know him from Adam — I scarcely looked at him. Mrs. Ubbard gave me a loaf and I nipped back to my own place. I took her a new loaf back next morning when the baker came his rounds, but her door was locked. And I've never seen her since, so I conclude she went away early that day. She did use to go away sometimes."

"You've known Mrs. Ubbard some time I suppose, missus?" asked Stell.

"Some years — seven or eight — ever since I came to live here," replied the woman. "She was here — same house — when we came."

"What sort of woman is she, now?" enquired Stell.

"Oh, well, you know, Mr. Stell, she's a queer 'un! They do say — she used to let her tongue go a bit sometimes — they do say that she'd been a real, proper actress once upon a time, and had come down in the world. You see, Mr. Stell, it's this way — she can't keep off the bottle! Gin! She's never what they call intoxicated, drunk you know, but she's — well, sodden with it. Oh, she's a queer old party, is Mrs. Ubbard — Mother Ubbard as they call her. But of course all that's between you and me, Mr. Stell."

"Oh, of course," said Stell. "Well, good night, missus."

The woman said good night and went her way, and Stell went his, thinking. A young man at Mrs. Ubbard's, making notes in a little book? Could that have been Clegg? If so, where was the little book? He hurried to his lodgings, swallowed his supper, and returned to the centre of the town, in search of Marston.

Marston, unearthed late at night at a friend's house, listened wonderingly to Stell's story.

"Everything that was found in Clegg's pockets is in a sealed parcel at my office," he said when Stell had finished. "We'll examine the lot the first thing tomorrow morning. But look here, Stell — do you come down in the morning, drop in at the theatre and find out what they know about Mrs. Ubbard — when she was last there, and so on. If that was really Clegg who was with her that evening — "

"If we find the notebook the woman told me of amongst the things taken from Clegg's clothing," interrupted Stell, "it was Clegg!"

"Well, we'll see — in the morning," said Marston. "But find out what you can at the theatre. There'll be somebody there, caretaker or something of that sort, who'll know."

Stell called in at the theatre next morning and with some difficulty unearthed a sort of general utility man who could answer his questions.

"Mother Ubbard!" said this person. "She ain't been here these last few days. I sent a boy round to see what was amiss, but he couldn't get no answer. Got hold of a fresh bottle o' comfort, I should say, guv'nor — when she starts on that game you don't see her no more till she's had her whack!"

"I should think one bottle wouldn't last very long if she's that sort," suggested Stell.

"Well, I mean in a way o' speaking, guv'nor. What I mean is that if she gets hold of a bit of extra money, like, she goes on the booze. And when Mother Ubbard's on the loose she ain't going to scrub floors and shake carpets, d'ye see? She's very high and mighty when she's on the booze, Mother Ubbard is — takes to spouting Shakespeare and such like, same as if she was one o' them there tragedy queens. Which she says she was, once upon a time. And what might you be wanting with Mother Ubbard, guv'nor?"

Stell did not enlighten this inquisitive person: instead, he went on to Marston's office; Marston had just arrived and was unlocking his safe. He produced a sealed parcel and placed it on a table before the detective.

"Everything's in there," he said. "Look for yourself."

Stell undid the wrappings of the parcel and turned over the contents. There was little to examine. A cheap watch and chain, a handful of loose silver, mingled with a few coppers, a knife, a pencil or two, a paper packet of cigarettes, a box of matches — these were things he would have expected to find on a young fellow like Clegg. But there was what the woman of Simpson's Yard would have called a little book — a cheap memorandum book, ruled with cash lines. Half of it was filled with particulars of Clegg's expenditure, but here and there were some entries in shorthand. The last used page, in the middle of the book, was covered with shorthand.

"I'll lay a thousand to one it was Clegg that the woman I spoke to last night saw in Mrs. Ubbard's cottage!" exclaimed Stell. "He'd gone there for the same purpose that took him to Mrs. Milford's — to collect evidence! No doubt this is a note of what he got out of Mrs. Ubbard. But I can't read it. I know some shorthand, but not this stuff. Must be a system of his own."

"Stell!" said Marston. "We ought to have a look at Mrs. Ubbard's cottage! Inside, I mean. How do we know she's gone away? She — may be there. Anyhow, we'll see. Come back in an hour, and we'll go up to Simpson's Yard."

Stell went away, but he spent his hour of waiting to some profit, in his own opinion. He made for the chemist's shop into which Clegg had been carried when he collapsed in the street, and finding him in, got the chemist aside.

"I want to ask you a question," he said. "Between ourselves, you know. You remember that Clegg's body was brought in here when he fell outside your shop?"

"Not likely to forget it!" replied the chemist.

"You were, practically, the first to examine it?"

"I was — if you call that an examination. I took a close look at him, felt his pulse, heart, and that sort of thing. He was dead then — dead enough."

"Did you notice anything about him, now?" asked Stell. "What I really want to know is this — did you notice any particular odour about his lips?"

The chemist smiled.

"Well, I did," he said frankly. "I drew the attention of the doctors to it when they came.

"What was it?"

"Gin! Just that — gin! He'd certainly been drinking gin not so very long before he collapsed."

"The doctors say positively that he was poisoned," said Stell.

"No doubt about that! And I should say the poison had been put into the gin he drank.

I should have no doubt about that either!"

Stell went back to Marston. Marston had already sent two plainclothes men up to the neighbourhood of Simpson's Yard. He and Stell followed. With as little show of force as possible they broke into Mrs. Ubbard's cottage. Marston, entering first, turned into the open door of the living room. A sharp exclamation broke from him.

"Just what I thought might be possible!" he said, half-retreating on the others. "She's here — look!"

Stell looked past him. Mrs. Ubbard was there — lying back in an old easy chair that stood by the hearth. It needed but one glance at her rigid figure, grey face, and open mouth to see that she was dead.

"Pull up that blind!" said Marston.

In the light that streamed in as one of the plainclothes men drew up the thick blind Stell's eyes ran over the various objects in the little room. He pounced at once on one. There, in the middle of the table, stood a bottle of gin — half-empty. Near it were two glasses. One was entirely empty; the other held about a half-inch of fluid; it stood nearest to Mrs. Ubbard's chair.

Stell had already told Marston of his visit to the chemist's, and the Superintendent knew well enough why the detective seized bottle and glasses and set them aside for removal. If there was poison in that bottle of gin, and traces of it in the glasses, why then —

A policeman in uniform rode up to the door of the cottage on a bicycle, and catching sight of one of the plainclothes men, called to him.

"Is the Superintendent there?"

Marston hurried out. The policeman got off his bicycle and came up.

"Mr. Braithwaite's at your office, sir," he said. "He's just arrived from abroad and he says he ought to see you at once."

"Tell him I'll come down immediately," replied Marston. "And here — you know where Alderman Wardle's warehouse is? Go there and tell him I want to see him at the City Hall, as soon as he can get there, and he's to bring Mr. Withers with him."

The policeman saluted and went off, and Marston called Stell outside.

"Braithwaite's come!" he said. "He wants to see us at once. Bring that bottle and the glasses."

Then he gave some orders and directions to the two plainclothes men, and going out of Simpson's Yard hailed a taxi cab in the main road and went off with Stell and his discoveries. A hurried ride through the streets, a brief call at the City Analyst's, and within a quarter of an hour he, Stell, Withers, Wardle, and Braithwaite were closeted together in his room.

Braithwaite, a sharp-eyed, alert, youngish man, of great repute in the town, had obviously formed certain conclusions of his own during his journey from Barcelona, and was prepared to submit them. But first he wanted to know what the Mayor had already told Marston. Marston repeated the Mayor's story.

"Yes," said Braithwaite. "That's quite correct — up to the point where the Mayor left me and Riversley together. But after that the conversation became more intimate. He told me a good deal. Now listen — are there any particular questions that have suggested themselves to you since you heard what the Mayor had to say? There are? Well, what, now?"

"To start with," said Marston, "did Sir John Riversley tell you that one reason why he wished to alter his will was that a beneficiary under the first will had deceived him?"

"He did," replied Braithwaite. "He said as much as that to me and the Mayor, before the Mayor left us. He said it again to me, in a more emphatic fashion."

"Well, here's a most important question. Did he tell you who it was that had deceived him?"

"Yes! His manager, Carroll!"

"Actually told you his name?"

"He did! Carroll!"

"Did he tell you anything further about Carroll? Who he really was? — or anything of that sort?"

"Yes — he talked pretty freely about him. He said that Carroll was the son of an old actor friend of his who'd died leaving this lad friendless and penniless. He, Riversley, in some return for a former kindness done him by the father, had educated him at his own cost, and eventually finding that he was a clever young fellow and particularly good at figures and finance had sent him to Cambridge with a view of making him his business manager. In due course this had been done, and he had trusted him implicitly. Recently, however, he had discovered some discrepancies in the accounts, and he had now sent for his solicitor, Mr. Withers, and when he arrived was going to get a chartered accountant to go through the books."

"Did he tell you if Carroll knew of this?"

"He said he'd spoken to Carroll about it, but had not told him the full extent of his discoveries. He had, however, told him that if he found there was anything wrong, he, Carroll, would have to go."

"Well, just one more question, Mr. Braithwaite. It's a highly important one. Sir John Riversley mentioned his securities to you, didn't he? But — did he tell you where they were?"

"Yes! He told me it was a peculiarity of his to carry his securities with him wherever he went. In fact, he showed me where they were — in a black despatch case which stood on the table in the private room in which we had our interview. But, he said, he'd determined to lodge them with his bankers here in Hatherford."

Marston turned to the other men, who had listened in silence.

"There's no doubt about — my mind!" he exclaimed. "I must get a warrant for Carroll's arrest!"

Chapter 23

WHO BOUGHT IT?

WARDLE and the two solicitors went away soon after this, and Marston turned to Stell.

"Now, Stell," he said, "what do you suggest? But first of all, do you know if Carroll is still at Mrs. Milford's?"

"He was there when I last heard of him," replied Stell.

"Well," continued Marston, "we've enough information to justify us in getting a warrant for him, but it might perhaps be better if we got him here or saw him at his lodgings and questioned him a bit. What do you think?"

"I suggest seeing him at Mrs. Milford's," said Stell. "From all I've seen of him, and heard about him, this will take him aback. If we tell him that we want some information about himself from his own lips, in consequence of something we've heard, he'll probably give himself away in some fashion. But — it had better be done at once." Marston glanced at his watch.

"See if Robertshaw and Morgan are about," he said. "I can't go up there before noon, but we can at least have the place watched until then."

Stell went out and came back presently with the two plain-clothes men who had once kept watch on Macdermott, and lost him.

"Look here, you two," said Marston. "I want you to go up to Thornholme Street. Do you know — either of you — Mrs. Milford's house? Both? Very well, there's a man named Carroll staying there — Sir John Riversley's business manager. You know him, by sight? Very good. Now I don't want him to slip through your fingers as Macdermott did! Remember, there are back doors to those houses in Thornholme Street. One of you keep an eye on the front door; the other on the back. If Carroll should leave the house, follow him. I shall be up there before long."

The men went away, and Marston gathered up some papers from his desk and made for the door.

"I've got to attend the borough Court, Stell," he said. "You meet me at the corner of Thornholme Street at a quarter-past twelve."

He hurried off, and Stell presently left the police station and went out into the town. But before leaving he turned into a certain room, close to Marston's, in which he had a cupboard wherein he kept things that he desired to take particular care of: that cupboard was fitted with a patent lock, and the key never went out of Stell's keeping. In this cupboard, on returning from Mrs. Ubbard's cottage, he had placed the bottle of gin and the glasses which he had found on the old woman's table; now he repossessed himself of them, having two intentions in mind. One was to take bottle and glasses to the City Analyst with a view of ascertaining if there was poison in the gin and traces or evidences of it in the glasses. But the other was somewhat different. Stell, when he first saw and handled the bottle, had at once noticed that it had been bought at a certain tavern adjoining the Theatre Royal, the landlord of which, in addition to being a publican and licensed victualler, was also the proprietor of a wine and spirit business. There was his label on the bottle

— Nicholas Ramsdale, Wine and Spirit Merchant, Prince of Wales's Hotel, Coldingham Road, Hatherford. Excellent! — for Stell's purposes: he wanted to ask Mr. Ramsdale a question. And when he had visited the City Analyst and delivered up bottle and glasses and told their history, he headed in Mr. Ramsdale's direction.

Mr. Ramsdale was behind the counter in his bottle department when Stell entered. He knew Stell and gave him a cheery greeting. Stell responded with a meaningful look.

"A word with you!" he said.

Ramsdale was quick to understand He motioned the detective into a private parlour at the back of the shop, and following him inside, shut the door.

"What now, my boy?" he asked cheerily. "Anything I can do in your line? Not my line, my boy, but always willing to assist in the cause of justice, eh?"

"You may be able to give me some material assistance," responded Stell. "But it's all between ourselves, you know."

"Oh, to be sure, my boy!" assented Ramsdale. "Absolutely sub rosa, my boy — as the scholars say, I believe. And what is it, my boy?"

"Seeing that you're next to next door to the Theatre Royal," said Stell, "I daresay you know no end of these theatrical folks."

"Bushels of 'em, my boy!" replied Ramsdale confidently. "I make bold to say, my boy, that there's scarcely a Thespian come to this town for the last twenty years who hasn't made my acquaintance! Being, as you say, my boy, in contiguity to the T. R."

"Do you know Carroll, business manager to Sir John Riversley?" asked Stell, bluntly.

"Do I know Carroll, my boy? As well as I know you," answered Ramsdale. "A regular customer of mine, my boy — since he came to the town."

"What sort of a customer?" asked Stell. "I mean — here or in the tavern?"

"Well, the tavern — saloon bar, you know, my boy," replied Ramsdale. "Drops in for his little drop of comfort and refreshment occasionally, as they all do."

"Look here!" said Stell. "Has Carroll ever bought bottles of spirits from you?"

"Has Carroll ever bought bottles of spirits from me, my boy? Frequently, my boy, oh, frequently!" answered Ramsdale.

"What?" demanded Stell.

"What, my boy? Whisky," replied Ramsdale. "Whisky! — of the variety called Scotch."

"Just crystallise that memory of yours!" said Stell, admonishingly. "Now listen! — has he ever — recently — bought a bottle of gin from you?"

Ramsdale clasped a fat hand to his forehead. Obviously, he thought — hard.

"Ah!" he exclaimed suddenly. "Yes, my boy! I remember it, for a simple reason. It was sweet gin — the sort that the women like, my boy! Men, of course, like their gin dry. But the ladies, my boy — "

"When was this?" asked Stell.

"A few nights ago, my boy," replied Ramsdale. "Early in the evening. I remember now — he said it must be sweet."

"Would your label be on the bottle?" enquired Stell.

"Of a surety, my boy! All my bottles bear my label," said Ramsdale. "And very pretty labels, too — nice bit of colour printing."

Stell turned to the door.

"Thank you," he said. "Greatly obliged!"

"Very welcome, my boy," replied Ramsdale. "But if the talking's done — and you observe, my boy, that I ask no questions! — what do you say to a little heart-freshener, my boy? Give it a name!"

"Not even a spoonful of ginger beer!" answered Stell with a laugh. "Got big business on, Ramsdale. Look in this evening's papers."

He went away then — to make the end of Thornholme Street by a roundabout route. And as he went, he reflected. His reflections were really in the form of a question. Did Carroll take that bottle of gin to Mrs. Ubbard's? If he did . . .

Before Stell reached the end of Thornholme Street at which he was to meet Marston, Marston came along from the town in a taxicab. He had two men in plain clothes with him in whom Stell recognised two of his fellow detectives. Marston, catching sight of Stell, stopped the cab and got out.

"These two?" he said, as Stell approached him. "Where had we better put them to wait? Top of the street?" He turned, putting his head into the cab. "Go up to the top of Thornholme Street, you two," he continued. "Wait in the cab round the corner till Stell fetches you: don't show yourselves till then."

The cab moved off; Stell drew Marston aside.

"I've found out a certain something," he said. "You know the bottle of gin which I took from the old woman's table this morning? Well, I've traced its sale. It was bought a few evenings ago, from Ramsdale at the Prince of Wales's Hotel, close by the Theatre Royal, by — Carroll!"

Marston pursed his lips to a whistle of astonishment.

"Whew!" he exclaimed. "Is that certain, Stell?"

"Dead certain!" said Stell. "He was particular, Carroll, that it should be sweet gin — the sort women like."

"Well, well!" said Marston. "That's a remarkable discovery! I say — that's just the thing we can tackle him on first! We'll see what he has to say to that. It'll lead on to other matters. Come on — " we'll go straight to the house."

Thornholme Street, being nothing but a street of lodging houses, was quiet enough when the two men turned into it. But at the top, lounging about, was Robertshaw. He came slowly down the street as Marston and Stell walked up it, and passing them without a stop or any recognition, murmured a few words as his sleeve brushed the detective's.

"Seen nothing so far!"

"Keep about!" responded Marston without as much as a glance of recognition. "We may want you at once."

He and Stell went on in silence — to the front door of Mrs. Milford's house. A first ring of her bell brought no immediate response; at the second the door was opened by a girl, chiefly noticeable for her mop of violently red hair, who stared wide-eyed at the two men.

"Mrs. Milford in?" asked Marston.

"Mrs. Milford's out," replied the red-haired one. "She's gone to see a lady at the hospital what's been took very bad."

"Ah!" said Marston. "Well — is Mr. Carroll still here?"

"He's in. Might you be wanting of him?"

As a proof that this was precisely what he did want, Marston stepped inside, and the girl, retreating, opened a door. The two visitors got a vision of Carroll, in his shirt sleeves, busily engaged in packing a portmanteau. He looked round — and Stell was quick to notice that if he showed some surprise, he also showed no concern. And he was the first to speak.

"Hullo!" he exclaimed. "What brings you two here? Any fresh news?"

Marston walked into the room, followed by Stell. Stell left both doors open: street door and parlour door; he might want to go out hurriedly.

"Leaving us, Mr. Carroll?" asked Marston.

"This afternoon," replied Carroll. "I've wound everything up now, so there's no need to remain here longer. Unless, of course, you want me for anything."

"Well, we do want you — for something," said Marston, with a sly smile. "We — to begin with — want you to answer a few questions."

Carroll, busy with the portmanteau, which lay open on the centre table of the parlour, did not look round from his task. He was busy in folding and arranging clothes, and he went on with his job, as if the visit of Marston and Stell was of no particular moment.

"Yes?" he said. "Fire ahead, then? What do you want to know? Though I think I've told you everything I know already."

"Not quite all, perhaps," replied Marston. "However, we'll come to facts. We just want a little information regarding certain things — facts, in fact! — which have come to our knowledge. To begin with, you bought a bottle of gin a few evenings ago, from Ramsdale, at the Prince of Wales's Hotel, didn't you?"

Carroll turned sharply. For the first time a look of — what was it, wonder or suspicion? — crossed his face. Not suspicion, decided Stell — no, wonder.

"A bottle of gin — at Ramsdale's?" he exclaimed. "Well, now I come to think of it, I did! Bit of an unusual purchase for me — I don't drink gin. Bought plenty of bottles of whisky from Ramsdale, but never a bottle of gin before. But — what's all this about?"

"What did you do with that bottle of gin?" asked Marston.

"Do with it? I — "Carroll suddenly paused; the look on his face changed to one of undeniable suspicion. "Look here!" he exclaimed. "What are you two after? What's it got to do with you that I bought a bottle of gin at Ramsdale's? Why do you ask what I did with it?"

Marston remained silent for a moment. Then he looked at Stell. And Stell nodded — silently.

"Well, I'll tell you," said Marston. "You know that the young fellow Clegg died suddenly in the street a few evenings ago, and that his death was due to poison. We've ascertained that Clegg, a short time before his death, was at the house of the old theatre charwoman, Mrs. Ubbard. Mrs. Ubbard had not been seen by neighbours since the night of Clegg's death, and this morning we broke into her house. We found her dead, and she'd been dead some days, too! And on the table was a bottle of gin which had been bought from Ramsdale, and we believe it to be the bottle you bought. So — "

He paused suddenly. Carroll, whose expression had changed from one of suspicion to one of blank astonishment, let out a sharp exclamation.

"Good God!"

"What have you got to say about it, Mr. Carroll?" asked Marston.

Carroll, who was standing with his hands in his pockets, staring at his questioner, pulled himself erect and set his jaw.

"Nothing!" he replied firmly. "Nothing at all!"

"I think you'd better," said Marston.

"Then you think wrongly," retorted Carroll. "I shall not say one word — now! Is that all you've got to say?"

"No, it isn't," replied Marston. "I've a good deal more to say. We've had information this morning that Sir John Riversley just before his death — his murder, I should say — had discovered a discrepancy in your accounts — "

"That's a damned lie!" exclaimed Carroll. "He never discovered anything of the sort. There is nothing of the sort! You can have my accounts examined, ever since I became manager, by all the chartered accountants in England, and you'll not find a flaw in them. Sir John and I had a difference as to certain payments, and as to certain methods of accountancy, but that's all. My books, sir, are open to anybody's inspection. And what's all this about, pray? Are you accusing me of killing Riversley — and Clegg, too? Come?"

Chapter 24

THE RED-HAIRED GIRL

THERE was something so positive about Carroll's manner and tone that the two police officials, taken aback, turned to each other with enquiring looks. Was all this bluff? — or was it the indignation of conscious innocence. Before either could speak, Carroll went on, more indignantly than before.

"I've told you from the beginning — and a dozen or twenty times since! — that I know nothing whatever about Riversley's murder," he said. "And as to Clegg's — if it was murder — I know less; I don't think I've ever seen Clegg except in the box office on the day we opened here — I was scarcely ever in his way after that. And if you've got some bee in your bonnet about my accounts with Riversley, I can't help it! He'd one himself — that's true, but — "

"You admit there was some dispute between you?" interrupted Marston.

"I've just said so — if you like to call it a dispute. It was a question of accountancy. My books are all right, anyhow!"

"Where are your books?" enquired Marston. "Here? Available?"

"No — they were sent yesterday to the firm in London that's always examined them on Sir John's behalf. They'll testify as to their being all right. Riversley, I say, got a bee in his bonnet about them — he was a keen man about money, but he knew nothing about finance. Good Lord! — he couldn't have told you what two-sixteenths of a pound amounts to!"

"Mr. Carroll!" said Marston. "You would save us and yourself a lot of trouble if you'd answer a simple question! I've asked it already and I'll ask it again. What did you do with that bottle of gin you bought from Ramsdale?"

"I shan't answer your question!" declared Carroll. "I've said so before."

"You could answer it, then — if you liked?"

"I could do a lot of things — if I liked! In this case — I don't like."

"Suppose I tell you that you'd better?"

"That sounds like a threat! Is it a threat?"

Marston paused for a moment's reflection. After all, Carroll might be bluffing them to gain time. Then Marston made up his mind.

"I'd better be candid with you," he said. "I've got a warrant for you in my pocket, and a search warrant, too. You see, we've had certain information. If you'd answered my questions — told me more, eh?"

"I shall not answer that question!" said Carroll, doggedly. "And if you arrest me, it'll be at your peril — "

"No peril, Mr. Carroll! You ought to know better than that. There's ground for suspicion against you, and we shall have to clear things up. Stell! — call those two officers in! Mr. Carroll, you'll have to go down to the police station — I'll read the warrant to you there. And — "

Stell had moved towards the half-opened door while Marston was talking. Before he could reach it, the red-haired girl burst into the room. Her eyes blazed, an angry colour lit up her freckled cheeks; she looked half a fury as she burst out into shrill, passionate speech.

"I was listening at the door!" she shouted. "I knew what you were — police! Don't you go with them, Mr. Carroll! I know all about that bottle of gin!" She turned, panting, on Marston. "I can tell you what he did with it!" she went on. "He bought it for — "

With a sudden cry of dismay Carroll darted at the girl, and seizing her round the shoulders with one hand, clapped the other over her mouth.

"Shut up, you damned fool!" he cried. "Hold your tongue —"

"Let that girl go, Mr. Carroll!" exclaimed Marston. "Take your hand away from her mouth. Let her speak!"

"You be damned!" retorted Carroll savagely. He was still holding the struggling girl in a tight grip, and now he began to force her backwards out of the room. "Shut up and be quiet, I tell you!" he went on as she struggled to free herself. "Get out and hold your tongue — you're making matters worse — ah!"

The red-haired girl, well-built and muscular, suddenly wrenched herself free, and clapping a hand to her bosom, backed away from Carroll, panting for breath. She gave Carroll a look.

"Good God!" muttered Stell. "She's in love with him!"

"Speak, my lass, if you want to!" said Marston. "Keep your hands off her, Mr. Carroll. Now, my lass?"

The girl got her breath.

"I will speak!" she said. "I won't see him taken off to prison for what he never did! He bought that gin for the mistress, and I saw him give it to her. And the mistress took it to Mother Ubbard's!"

Marston let out a sharp exclamation of astonishment at the same time that Carroll made one of despair. Before either could speak, a sound in the street outside made Stell turn to the window. He, too, uttered a sharp word of surprise.

“Here’s Mr. Jubb!” he exclaimed. “Come in a taxi! — he looks as if he’d something to tell, too!”

Chapter 25

RECALLED!

MARSTON turned to the window. There was a taxi cab drawn up outside the house, and Jubb was saying something to its driver, alternating his speech with glances at Mrs. Milford's windows. Marston turned to Carroll and the still panting girl.

"Mr. Carroll, I'll trust to your honour not to leave this room," he said. "You, my girl, go back to your kitchen, and wait till I can speak to you. Stell! — fetch Mr. Jubb in, and take him into that room on the other side of the passage. Now, Mr. Carroll — you'll stay here?"

"I'll stay here!" replied Carroll. "The thing's done! You've got it!"

Marston looked at him a moment as if to ask what he meant; then he shook his head and went out of the room. Stell had already gone and was now ushering in Jubb.

Jubb was obviously in a state of high excitement. He came bustling in, calling for Marston; Marston hurried him into a room opposite to that in which he had left Carroll, and closed the door on themselves and Stell.

"Something happened, Mr. Jubb?" he asked.

"Something happened?" exclaimed Jubb. "I should think something has happened! I've raced here like — like anything! — to tell you. Went down to the City Hall first — they said you'd come up here. I say! — what d'ye think? Mrs. Wollaton's spoken!"

"You mean — got her memory back?" asked Marston. "When? How?"

"I'll tell you," responded Jubb. He pulled out a handkerchief and mopped his forehead. "Whew! How I've raced here! Well, it was this way. My wife mentioned to me this morning that she and Wollaton were going to see Mrs. Wollaton at that nursing home, and as I'd nothing particular to do, I said I'd go with them. So we all went — in my car. We found Mrs. Wollaton, with a nurse, on a verandah, in front of the house, enjoying the sunshine. She was just as she'd always been since I first saw her there — quiet. You've not seen her at the nursing home?"

"No," replied Marston.

"I have!" said Stell.

"Then you'll know what I mean — how she'd sit looking at you as if — well, as if she didn't at all mind your being there, and so on, but hadn't the ghost of a notion who you were. Pretty much as if you and she were all strangers, meeting in a hotel lounge; that sort of thing. Well, I tell you, we were all sitting with her there, on the verandah, when a woman suddenly came round the corner from the entrance gates: a visitor, evidently. And by Jove! Who do you think the woman was!" continued Jubb, sinking his voice. "Why, the woman who lives here — Mrs. Milford! I know her well enough — wardrobe-keeper at the Theatre Royal now, but she used to be a pretty well-known actress, once. Yes, sir, Mrs. Milford!"

"Well?" demanded Marston.

"Well, I happened to glance from Mrs. Milford (to whom, of course, I'd nodded as she came by) to Mrs. Wollaton. Mrs. Wollaton's face was — good Heavens! I don't know what it was, or expressed. It was — queer! Her eyes were starting — her lips were opening — it was as if — as if she was trying to — I don't know what! Think, I suppose. But anyhow, as Mrs. Milford disappeared inside the house and closed the door, Mrs.

Wollaton let out the most awful scream I ever heard in my life — I'll dream of that for many a month, I know! Then — she fainted!"

"Straight off — without a word?" asked Marston.

"Straight off — then and there — without a word! But the nurse was close by, and she had a doctor there in a minute or two from inside the house. They brought her to. First person she recognised was Wollaton. She began to cry when she saw him — by Heavens, sirs, it was a painful situation, for she didn't know Wollaton from Adam five minutes before. Well, Wollaton soothed her wonderfully — and she remembered me, next. Gad! — her memory had come back! And after a bit, when the doctor and the nurse had fixed her all right, though she was, of course, queer and trembling, she told what she remembered. About that night at the theatre, you understand?"

The two listeners nodded silently. Each was wondering if the truth was coming out, at last.

"Briefly, it comes to this," continued Jubb. "She says she followed Riversley to Hatherford from London, to get a clear understanding with him about — something. She saw him on the Monday afternoon: he told her to come to his dressing room at the theatre at night, and how to reach it by the side door. She followed his instructions. She got into the passage that led to the door of his room; the door was slightly open. She looked in. Riversley was bending forward over his table. Through a door at the other side of the room a woman was vanishing, who carried a small black box or case. The woman looked back for a second — Mrs. Wollaton saw her face distinctly. Then she disappeared. Mrs. Wollaton went in. Riversley never moved. She went up to him — and saw he was dead! And after that, she remembered no more until — until she saw the woman again! And, look here, you two, the woman is — "

Stell, who was standing by the window, suddenly lifted his hand.

"'Sh!" he said warningly. "She's here!"

The other two looked out. Mrs. Milford was approaching the house from the opposite side of the street.

Chapter 26

I'LL TELL!

MARSTON turned quickly to Jubb with a sharp question.

"Does she know anything of what you've just told us — about Mrs. Wollaton?"

"Nothing!" replied Jubb. "She'd gone into the nursing home — gone inside, you know."

Marston motioned Stell to the door.

"Meet her, Stell!" he said. "Bring her in here!"

Stell went out into the hall. The front door stood wide open, and Mrs. Milford was coming up the steps to it. At sight of the detective she paused, staring and frowning at him.

"Hullo?" she exclaimed. "What are you doing here? What do you want?"

"Just a little matter of business, Mrs. Milford," replied Stell. "The Superintendent's here, too — he'd like a word with you. This way, if you please."

He shepherded her carefully into the room which he had just left, and closing the door, planted himself with his back to it. Mrs. Milford, a little in advance of him, paused again and stared again.

"What's the meaning of this, Mr. Marston?" she demanded. "What do you want here? It seems a strange thing to walk into my house when I'm not — "

"You have other people in your house, Mrs. Milford," interrupted Marston. "You've Mr. Carroll, for instance. We came to see him."

Mrs. Milford was carrying a small basket. The three men glanced at it as she set it down on the table. Fruit — flowers; innocent things. Clearly, she had not anticipated.

"What do you want with Mr. Carroll?" she asked. "And isn't he in? — haven't you seen him?"

"We've seen him," replied Marston. "Mr. Carroll is in the opposite room. The fact is, Mrs. Milford, I've got a warrant for his arrest — and a search warrant for this house as well. We were just about to remove Mr. Carroll when we saw you coming. You see — "

Mrs. Milford sat down in the nearest chair. She caught her breath in a short gasp.

"What — what is it?" she asked. "What — what are you charging him with?"

"You can guess, Mrs. Milford," said Marston. "There have been three deaths — murders, to use plain language — very lately. And we've certain evidence — "

He stopped abruptly. Mrs. Milford lifted a hand.

"Wait a minute!" she said. "What does Carroll say?"

"Nothing!" replied Marston. "But he knows something. Now — "

Again Mrs. Milford stopped him. She sat staring — at nothing — for a full moment, and then suddenly turned to Marston.

"Mr. Marston, let me have a word with you in private!" she said. "Send these other two away. No, I won't have that man here!" she went on, pointing to Stell. "You yourself, only. Send them out!"

Jubb left the room without further ado; Marston whispered a word or two to Stell.

"Stay outside, between the two doors!" he said. "Take care that Carroll doesn't leave, and that the girl doesn't go out."

Stell went, and Marston turned to Mrs. Milford. She had drawn off her gloves and now sat smoothing out the fingers. Instead of looking at Marston she kept her eyes on the gloves. After a brief silence, she spoke, in a queer, constrained voice.

"Mr. Marston! Are you suspecting Carroll of killing Riversley — and getting rid of the old woman and the boy?"

Marston was taken aback by this direct question. But after a brief reflection he decided to answer it in plain words.

"We have some very strong evidence that gives us ground for suspicion, Mrs. Milford," he said. "Enough to warrant us — "

"You're all wrong!" she broke in almost impatiently. "Carroll knows nothing whatever about Riversley's death, nor about the other two, either! He's as innocent as a child. I tell you, he knows nothing!"

"Do you?" asked Marston.

For the first time since Stell and Jubb had left the room Mrs. Milford looked up. She gave her questioner a straight, direct glance.

"Yes!" she answered. "I know everything! And — and as it's come to this, which I never believed possible, for it's a puzzle to me how you could ever suspect Carroll, I'll tell you. I killed all three of them!"

Marston stood silent. The room, to him, seemed full of silence. He found himself staring at Mrs. Milford's fingers, smoothing out the grey gloves. After what he felt to be a long time he spoke — the words sounded almost foolish.

"Do you really mean that?"

"I've told you! I killed John Riversley — but I never meant to kill him. I did mean it in the case of the other two — they were in the way; and their lives — what were they? A drunken old woman and a silly, conceited young jackanapes. You see, they'd found out something — both of them — and they were putting their heads together. And so — they just had to be removed."

"About Sir John Riversley?" said Marston. "You said you never meant — "

"I never meant to kill him," she continued. "But I'm going to tell you all about it — it's got to be cleared up now, so that you'll have no suspicion about Carroll. It's this way, you see, Mr. Marston — I'm going to tell you everything. You see, though he doesn't know it, Carroll is my nephew. He's the son of a favourite sister of mine, with whom John Riversley was once very much in love, really and properly in love. She wouldn't have him — we knew too much of his character as a young man. She married another man; they both died when Carroll was a mere baby, leaving him unprovided for. I looked after him for years; then I got John Riversley to undertake his education. As a matter of fact, he adopted Carroll — on the strict condition that Carroll was not to know anything of his antecedents — he meant him, eventually, to take his name. In course of time he sent him to college, and then he made him his business manager. And as far as I know, everything was going on all right until John Riversley came to Hatherford — for the first and last time. Then he came to see me, and I found that everything was going wrong."

"When did he come to see you?" asked Marston.

"He came to see me on the Sunday afternoon, on his way to the hotel. He was full of complaints and grumblings. He said he'd found out that there was something wrong with Carroll's accounts, that Carroll was cheating him, and so on. He was in a nasty temper, and he declared that while he was here he'd make a new will, cut Carroll out of it, and in addition to that would get rid of him. Now, Mr. Marston, all that sounds very well, but I know — now — something at the back of it. The real truth was, or is, that there has lately been a certain young lady in Riversley's company — she wasn't here with it then — with whom he fell in love, only to find that she and Carroll were in love with each other. And John Riversley, ever since I knew him, was a mean, selfish man, who must be first — you understand? Well, this was his dirty way of having his revenge, and of damaging Carroll, too. He — "

"Come to that Monday evening — if you wish to tell about it," interrupted Marston.

"I do wish to tell about it. I knew what time Riversley would come to the theatre, and I kept a lookout for him. Soon after he came I slipped into his dressing room. His dresser hadn't come; he was alone, and he was already at his table, beginning to make up. I begged and entreated him to withdraw all he'd said the day before and not to do what he'd threatened. It was all no good — he was in a nastier and meaner temper than before. And — well, I'm a hot-tempered woman, Mr. Marston, and impulsive, too. There was that rapier lying handy. Before I knew what I was doing, I picked it up and ran it into him as he sat there! I never meant to kill him; I meant to give him a sharp wound, enough to stop him from playing for a bit. But . . . well, you know what happened! I realised it at once, and I snatched up his despatch box and went away. And as a matter of fact, that old woman, Ubbard, and the lad, Clegg, saw me coming from the direction of his room."

"You acknowledge that you — got rid of them?" said Marston.

"I did get rid of them! Clegg came here, that night he was found dead or dying in the street later on. He as good as told me that he and Mother Ubbard knew. But he had an idea that Carroll was my accomplice, and he wanted to blackmail us. I trifled with him. He left me to go to Mrs. Ubbard's house. I knew how to settle them! I got Carroll to get me a bottle of gin. When I'd got it, and had done what I wanted with it, I slipped down to Mother Ubbard's with it — I was in the habit of taking her a few comforts now and then. And of course, she and Clegg had some of the gin, and — but you know all about that. You see, Mr. Marston, they just had to be put aside!"

Marston stood staring at her. Suddenly, his thoughts turned to something practical. "Mrs. Milford! — you'll have to go with us! But — that despatch case of Sir John's? Where is it?"

Mrs. Milford got up from her chair. She laid her gloves on the table beside the basket full of fruit and flowers.

"I quite understand that I shall have to go with you," she said. "There's one satisfaction, however. John Riversley's will'll stand, and Carroll'll get what he was going to be robbed of. The despatch box? — yes, it's upstairs, Mr. Marston. I'll go up and get it for you; it's got John Riversley's papers in it. A minute..."

Marston was a man of politeness. He opened the door and let Mrs. Milford pass through. She went slowly up the stairs; he heard a door closed somewhere overhead. Then he turned to Stell. Stell looked at him questioningly. And Marston shook his head.

"She's told me everything!" he whispered. "She did it! Hush! — she'll be down again in a minute — she's gone for the despatch box. When she comes..."

But Mrs. Milford never came...

THE END

Visit our website to explore the list of great Golden Age books and sign up to our infrequent Newsletter to be told of our latest titles first:
www.oleanderpress.com/golden-age-crime

OREON titles in this series

Glory Adair and the Twenty-First Burr
Victor Lauriston – 9781915475206

The Tunnel Mystery
J.C. Lenehan – 9781915475190

Murder on the Marsh
John Ferguson – 9781915475183

The Fatal Five Minutes
R.A.J. Walling – 9781915475176

The Crime of a Christmas Toy
Henry Herman – 9781915475169

Death of an Editor
Vernon Loder – 9781915475152

Death on May Morning
Max Dalman – 9781915475145

The Hymn Tune Mystery
George A. Birmingham – 9781915475091

The Essex Murders
by Vernon Loder – 9781915475053

The Middle of Things
J.S. Fletcher – 9781915475060

The Boat Race Murder
R. E. Swartwout – 9781915475039

Murder at the College
Victor L. Whitechurch – 9781999900489

The Charing Cross Mystery
by J.S. Fletcher – 9781909349711

The Doctor of Pimlico
William Le Queux – 9781909349735

Who Killed Alfred Snowe?
by J. S. Fletcher – 9781915475015

The Yorkshire Moorland Mystery
by J. S. Fletcher – 9781999900472

Fatality in Fleet Street *
Christopher St John Sprigg – 9781909349759

* Free ePub & PDF on sign-up to the
OREON newsletter:

www.oleanderpress.com/golden-age-crime

Printed in Great Britain
by Amazon

21491317R00120